arnaud rykner

THE LAST TRAIN

translated by
sue boswell

THIS IS A SNUGGLY BOOK

Original Title: *Le Wagon*
Original Publisher: © Actes Sud, 2010
Translation Copyright © 2020 by Sue Boswell
All rights reserved.

ISBN: 978-1-64525-037-1

THE LAST TRAIN

ARNAUD RYKNER is a writer and academic. He has published eight novels, several of which have appeared in paperback including *Le Wagon* which won the Jean d'Heurs prize for historical fiction in 2011; he has also published two plays. In 2019 he was awarded a residency at Villa Kujoyama in Kyoto, a cultural centre run by the Institut Français, where he began work on his next novel. He is a Professor and Director of Research at the Sorbonne Nouvelle in Paris, and has also authored a dozen essays and edited many collected works. He was responsible for the critical edition of the theatrical works of Nathalie Sarraute in the prestigious Pléiade series, as well as those of various other modern authors (such as Marguerite Duras) or older works (Marivaux, Maeterlinck), in paperback collections. As a theatrical producer he has notably put on the works of Nathalie Sarraute, Maurice Maeterlinck and Bernard-Marie Koltès. He is a Visiting Professor at Rutgers University (NJ) and a Senior Research Fellow of the University of Durham (UK).

SUE BOSWELL studied French Language and Literature at UCL and for a time taught French at Goldsmiths University of London. She then moved into university administration, specialising in university external relations and communications. Later she became a translator for the Wiener Holocaust Library, where she met Arnaud Rykner when he came to give a talk on his novel *Le Wagon*, now translated by her into English as *The Last Train*. Sue lives with her husband, Colin Boswell, in London and Ouveillan, a village near Narbonne in the Languedoc.

SNUGGLY BOOKS

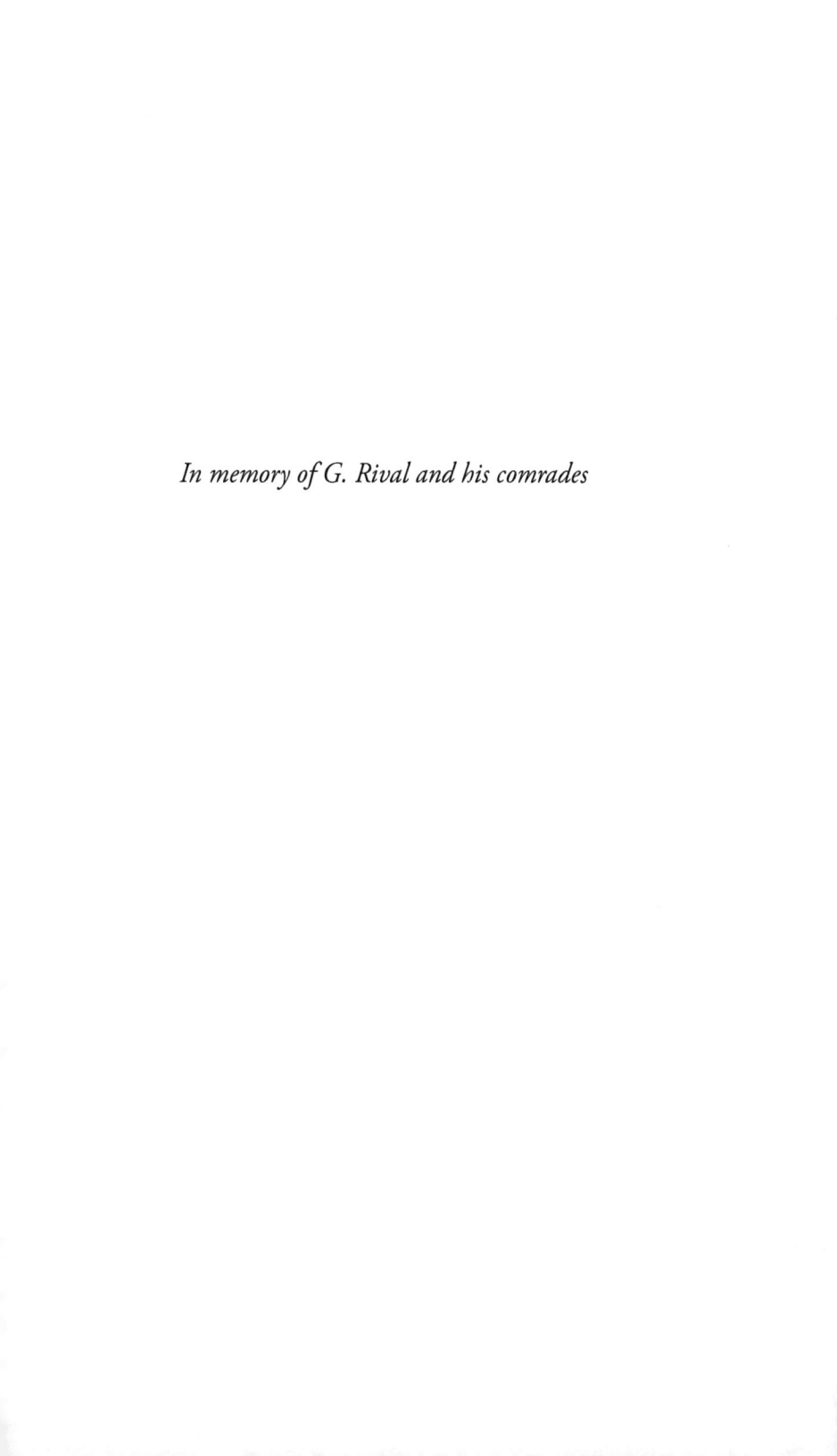

In memory of G. Rival and his comrades

And all the rest is literature.

—Paul Verlaine

THE LAST TRAIN

On 2 July 1944 one of the last trains of deportees left Compiègne.

The last train from Compiègne to Dachau.

But there were trains leaving France for the camps all through that summer. For a long time, and until the start of autumn, long after the Normandy landings, long after the liberation of Paris. As incredible as that may seem.

After their arrest by the French police or the Gestapo, two thousand and sixty-six men had been piled into this train, made up of twenty-two goods wagons, plus those holding the accompanying soldiers and a guard's van at the rear.

Many were members of the Resistance. Not all of them. Some were collaborators, some were informers. Others were nothing at all. Their crime had simply been to be in the wrong place at the wrong time.

The journey would have taken twenty-four hours under normal conditions; this convoy, number 7909, took more than three days, in blazing heat, through areas experiencing the highest temperatures ever recorded at that time. Conditions were such that seventy-seven hours after the *train left there were five hundred and thirty-six corpses—leaving only one thousand six hundred temporary survivors, many of whom would die without seeing France again.*

The great majority of the survivors would not speak about this experience for many years.

Until a historian came to ask them about it, almost to force them to speak. To help them to talk about their unbelievable experience in this train which came to be called, like a second-rate B-movie, 'The Death Train'.[1]

Amongst those who did speak about it, most seem to have left very little written testimony. Many never spoke of it again, saying nothing more about it than the few words required for that book.

❁

I would probably never have known anything about this train if someone I knew slightly had not told me about it one day. And about the fact that a member of my family had been there. And that around this fact there was silence, a lack of knowledge, a gaping, monstrous void. There was a missing link in a story connected to me and about which I had never known anything. I had always believed that this kind of void, this abyss, and yet an everyday event, only opened beneath the feet of others. Then, almost without my being aware of it, my body that day took the decision for me, that one day I would have to go beyond those few words exchanged during an apparently innocuous conver-

---

1 Christian Bernadac, *Le Train de la Mort*, Paris, éditions France-Empire, 1973, 367 pp.

sation. To go beyond and write about it, because writing has long been a necessity for me. Suddenly these two necessities became one—to write, and to seek what was missing over the course of time, the silence about one or more lives other than my own which seemed so slight in comparison.

At the same time I always knew that I should not write about it. That I did not have the right. And that I would do it even so. That I would restore the forbidden link.

I did not have the right, but I had to do it, and I have done it.

I no longer know whether it was some time before, or some time afterwards, that I learned another thing about which I cannot not speak—and about which I cannot speak. And not knowing made me understand what forgetting means, forgetting something so intense that the memory of it is no longer there, the order of events, what came before, what came after, the way truth is revealed and disorientates you so that you forget in what order it appeared and which is something of the truth itself.

So I decided to speak of this train.

And speaking of this train would mean speaking of that other forbidden thing.

Of that other story which is no longer my own. Which is also mine. Which is above all our common story.

I thought it was time, that even if I did not have the right to speak for another person I had to speak. To give a voice to the other. To take the place of the other. To lend the other my voice.

I had to try to do this terrible thing.

This story is true. Everything I have invented is also true. A sort of reality. It is not fiction.

I have said that a historian had done the research, reconstructed, rigorously and precisely interrogated people who were in the train and outside it. I have read all that, I did not wish to lie. I have read all I could so as not to misrepresent. Not to cheat. As far as possible.

But even knowing what I knew, reading what I had read, I could not help but lie. The unimaginable has to be imagined. Where you cannot form an image, an image has to be formed. A false image.

So all this is false. It is not a book about History. History is even worse.

Unreal.

This is a novel.

Wejn nischt, wejn nischt, klejner josem
Schpor dir trern chotsch dich kwelt, [. . .]
Schpor dir trern wi briljanten
Vest amol sej darfn sejr

—Mordechai Gebirtig

2 July.

In three days it's my birthday.

In three days' time I'll be twenty-two. The real start of life. The real end of childhood.

That's what I keep telling myself.

In three days' time, twenty-two.

The train rolls on; and this number in my head. Twenty-two. Twice eleven.

Eleven months ago my parents left. Eleven months later perhaps I shall be rejoining them.

Or maybe not.

I don't know what's in store for me.

I don't know what's in store for any us, crammed in so that we can hardly breathe. Crammed in like the animals we are not, that we don't want to be, that they won't force us to be. Or will they?

It's hard to think when your body is at the end of its tether, when hardly any air is circulating in your lungs, in your head, when the pressure in your head is like the pressure of the bodies in this wagon. Did my teachers know about that when they told us about the importance of the mind, of its superiority, of its transcendent splendour which persists despite everything? Or did they knowingly lie to us? Did their own war not teach them anything? Had they understood nothing? Or were they hiding from us what they had understood, as if the lie would keep hope alive.

They could only have dared to lull us with such soothing words if they had known nothing of feeling your neighbours' elbows in your ribs, your back, your belly, their unbearable smell, the constant pain, the noise of the wheels in your head, those wheels sawing into your head. I shall soon be twenty-two but I think I know more about it than all of them put together. And where are they now? How many are still alive? How many dead? How many are among the powerful, these conquerors who will soon be defeated taking us to who knows where, towards what scene of butchery? And how many are on our side?

There must be some like us.

They were not all full of arrogance and that putrid knowledge which stinks as badly as, or even worse than, the bodies pressing around me, crushing me. They were not all cowards and weaklings, they were not all vile, bludgeoning us with words they no longer believed in, which they could no longer believe in.

That's not possible.

Some were human beings. I want to believe that.

I want to believe it even if the jolting of the wagon reminds me of past beatings, even if the pressure of these bodies, these bones against mine, all this flesh that stinks so much you'd think it was already decomposing, even if all that hurts as much as the beatings. I want to believe that for some of them the words were not futile, that they did not use Homer, Rousseau, Hugo just to keep us quiet, to relish their power over us poor ignorant kids. There must be some of them on our side, there must be some who sincerely believed that their words could change the world, that their words were not empty words, that they did not lie, that they did not lie to us. I don't want to die just for having believed lies. Even if it stinks in here, even if stuff is dripping from everywhere, if it hurts to be so far from everything which kept me feeling alive, there must be some of them who believed, who told the truth when they said that our own survival depended on all those words, all those books we read, on the power of thought, the power of those words, and those looks which carried the weight of them. They can't all have lied!

But which of them would have imagined that a hundred bodies would be piled into a goods wagon intended for "forty men or eight horses crosswise"? And a hundred bodies in the wagon in front. And a hundred behind. And twenty wagons, or more, going where? Twenty wagons, one after the other like children being punished, shamefaced, snotty-nosed, beaten, dirty, holding up their pants, holding themselves in so as not to dirty their pants. Who could have predicted that we would be there tightening our bladders, praying that our bowels would not loosen, not straight away, not before we could find something other than this food tin that we pass around as best we can, this tin that we're nevertheless glad to have, this tin which stops us having to resort to using our own mess tins for that, this tin which splashes us with its filthy contents and which I have to try to empty out of the skylight.

Because fate would have it that I am next to one of the wagon's skylights, its opening enlarged by the removal of slats which had not been very firmly fixed. Somehow I arrived here, propelled by fate or the instinct for survival, a selfish but life-saving move which I had neither intended nor foreseen—so that I'm not even ashamed of it. It seems they've even taken shame away from us. Because this small opening with its barbed wire mesh might save my life. Who knows how long we can hold out in this suffocating dungeon, where there is so little air that some are fainting on their feet, where the heat is already unbearable less than an hour since leaving Compiègne. Too bad if it's down to me to empty the tin already overflowing with filth because of the lack of sanitation in the wagon, too bad if my hands stink. I know already how lucky I am to be here, even if I also know that I'll soon have to give up this place if I want to avoid becoming a totally selfish animal, obsessed by its own survival and nothing else. Perhaps those words from long ago will help me to do that. But already I'm having to bring them to mind, to repeat them to myself, to stop that animal taking over. At least they should help me to do that, not to give in too soon, to hold out a little bit longer.

Hold out? Stand up to what? To whom? For what? For whom? Longer than whom?

I shuffle aside as much as I can so that a comrade who has fainted can be passed through and with some difficulty hoisted up to the skylight. The sounds of moaning increase, the first arguments begin, presaging the worst in this intolerable closeness, this unbearable pressure of the other bodies which nevertheless enables us to keep upright despite the jolting of the train. In the midst of all this a voice is heard, an authoritative voice sure of itself when no one is sure of anything, and orders us to sit and stand in turn, so as to try to share the little remaining air.

"One half standing, the other sitting, starting from the left!"

Who said that?

For once, everyone is keen to obey. Everyone realises instinctively that this is our only hope of "holding out". We were no doubt waiting just for this voice to tell us what to do, to order us to stay alive. I inwardly bless this person who is still up to issuing orders.

What a strange ballet we are performing, as heaped upon each other we stand and sit in turn, as if on a spring, shared instinctively for the moment.

Sitting.

Standing.

Sitting.

Standing.

Sitting.

Standing.

When it's our turn to stand, even if our bodies are weary, the small current of hot air filtering through gives us a little courage. Our lungs expand, breathing the life-saving stink, the air circulating inside our heads just a little.

But when sitting, whilst our bodies may relax we are nearly asphyxiated.

It is infernally hot, infernally suffocating. What will it be like in the afternoon?

I used to enjoy blazing hot days like these with my brothers, when they were already so big and I was still small. Days when they took me in turn onto their shoulders and we jumped into the water, with them underneath and me on top. Days when it was good to feel hot, so as to enjoy the cold water even more.

But today there is no water, no wind. No brothers. Only fellow sufferers in misery.

It is too much for some of them, they try to stand up before their turn. It takes all the authority others can muster to maintain a semblance of order. How long is this going to go on? How long will we be able to bear the mounting horror inside us?

All that remains at the bottom of the small oil drum of water we were given at the station is a drop of steaming filthy liquid. It is so hot that despite our efforts to hold back, despite the discipline we have managed to keep, we have already drunk the little that wasn't spilled during the pushing and shoving at the beginning. My throat is horribly parched. I have never been so thirsty. And it can't even be ten o'clock yet.

The train is slowing down.

Is it a station?

I crane my neck towards the opening, trying to see out. My comrades ask, "Can you see anything?" No, I can't see a thing. There's nothing to see. A few trees. No roofs. No one here to help us. A voice whispers to me: "It seems to me we're going to hell." I would turn around to see who said this but I realise straight away that the voice is inside me. Perhaps this voice is all that's left. The voice that has been with me for years, the voice that always stops me falling, the voice that repeats to me the words I have learned, others' words I have learned over the years and that at first I thought served no purpose. All that remains to me of those days comes to me through that voice. All that remains to me of my childhood too. The voice of my parents, departed last year. The voice of my dead sister. The voice of my brothers who are perhaps hiding somewhere, maybe behind these trees—why not? My brothers coming to rescue me, my brothers waiting for the right moment to attack this train and rescue me.

But the train picks up speed and my brothers have not come.

At least with the train going again a little air gets in.

❋

Some people have taken advantage of the stop to throw out scraps of paper with their name on, and the name of someone to inform, a wife, a mother, a son. Where did they find something to write with? I never even thought of that.

But I can't get the thought of my brothers out of my head.

Apart from them, there is no one to miss me. That's something at least. No wife, no children. It's good for a man to be alone. That's something that should be taught to men when they're being sent to war. Perhaps I'm not yet sufficiently alone, since I can still think about my brothers.

Where are they now? I know that, like me, they've changed their names. Nothing left to give us away on the spot. But have they found a hiding place? And their children? I push that thought away. If I'm going to hold out at least for a few days I must forget everything, not think of them, not think of anyone, not my brothers and especially not my parents. Not think of anything except saving my own skin and the skin of the others it's rubbing against in this shared filth. As if I'd had to leave everything behind in that camp we departed from, perhaps never to return. As if I'd had to abandon everything: name, family, even my own memories.

I'm hot.

My head is swimming.

All around me there is moaning and groaning. This furnace is getting hotter. It must be over forty degrees in here. Are they not going to stop? Are they not going to open the doors, give us something to drink? After all, we're not animals. Or are we?

Several people have removed their shirts, just keeping their trousers on. I've done the same, even though the contact with all these bodies disgusts me, frightens me. My neighbour sees mine all covered in bruises from beatings. He looks into my eyes. He's already lost the ability to smile. But his look is enough for me. It's the look of one man to another, from one who is suffering to another who is suffering, from one who no doubt knows what a beating is even if his own body seems to be untouched. I lose myself in his gaze as if it could make him my brother. No need to speak. That will be something they've given to us—they'll have taught us how to be silent. How to be silent beneath their blows and beneath the comforting gaze of a friend. To keep silent about anything which doesn't need to be said and about anything which must remain hidden, buried, out of reach. That unsmiling gaze suddenly gave me strength to resist.

I don't remember ever being with so many half-naked men all in one room. If you can call it a room. Didn't have the chance for any training. My "basic training" was the war itself, soon lost. I should have told myself it was futile to get involved. But I believed I could "be useful" despite my age. Useful for what? For whom? For myself no doubt, more than for anyone. Useful . . .

I'm sitting again and take the chance to try to talk to my neighbour. When we're standing we have no strength for anything except breathing and trying to stay upright. Sitting, we try to forget that we're suffocating; we talk in undertones, not hearing everything the other says, not always hearing our own voice but, never mind, we're talking. That's something to hang on to, these words, despite the noise of the wheels, despite the comrades' moans and groans. My neighbour tells me he's a pharmacy student, that he was arrested in Paris in mid-May. He was counterfeiting papers. He told me— with humility? with bravado?—"less out of patriotism than out of the need to cock a snook at them." Like me, he was tortured, his back and thighs whipped to pieces with lead piping; but he tells me the wounds can sometimes heal. He himself hardly feels anything now. He says he was lucky, he should have been caught a lot earlier. He was known in his network as "the Baroness" so the Germans were looking for a woman. Unbelievable, they who are so methodical, so organised. So clever at hunting us out. It makes him laugh. I laugh with him. We both laugh quietly, despite being on the point of passing out.

We can still do that.

The strength to laugh at them, on the threshold of losing consciousness, perhaps soon on the threshold of the grave.

But it's our turn to stand. No more digressions. I wonder if I'll ever again have the opportunity for a laugh. Our expressions are set now. Only our mouths opening, as wide as they can. Like a diver coming out of the water.

The water.

Just the thought of it is painful, I'm so thirsty.

It would be better not to keep thinking. To think of nothing. To be nothing.

I'd rather be dead.

❃

I'm tired.

I must have dozed off for a moment. Shouting rouses me. A fight is starting.

I recognise Ladmiral's voice.

It was to be with him and his team that I changed groups on the way to the station, leaping from one group of a hundred to another. Fortunately the lads let me do it, one of them taking my place each time to keep the hundreds intact. I don't know what made me do it. I absolutely wanted to be with him. I'd got to know him in the lorry taking us from Fresnes to Royallieu. I was reassured on seeing him amongst us, as if his presence would benefit me, benefit all of us, and I did everything I could to join him. There was no sense to it, but I did it. I did it, in front of that anguished woman watching us in the empty streets of Compiègne. I did it in front of that child she made blow a kiss to the poor deportees. I did it because I could do it, to prove to myself that I could do it, and to give myself renewed courage by finding a leader.

I know he's a terrific sort. The chief of a resistance network. He was arrested with all his family. They could do nothing, not they for him nor he for them. But he's holding on. I don't know how he does that. I wonder where his wife and children are, what he must be feeling now; there are only men in our convoy. Will they be leaving too, on another train?

I realise that with some others he's trying to make a hole in the floor of the wagon. They must have kept knives on them. They didn't give in to the threats to shoot us all if a single piece of metal was found on a single one of us. They didn't obey the orders of that voice outside the wagon to throw anything out before the door was closed. They kept what they needed to make this attempt, this madness, magnificent and hopeless.

But some are against it. They're afraid of being killed if a single person gets away. They disgust me. As if we weren't going to die anyway. Ladmiral is right. Even before arriving at Compiègne we could have had a go, and those very people, or others—they're all the same—stopped us. Too afraid for their own rotten skins.

I feel bad judging them; I resent the hatred I feel whenever I see their cowardly faces. But I can't help it. The Germans have taken away from me any kindliness, any goodwill. That's what they've done to me. I can no longer forgive. Nothing. Nobody. If I get out of here alive, I shall have to learn it all again; but for now I don't want to try; I force myself not to try. It's necessary in order to hang on, not to become soft in my turn. Not to forgive. It is not true that forgiveness is what makes you human. To be human, to stay human, I have to hold on to the hatred, and not forgive. Not forgive anyone.

A sharper voice begs Ladmiral's men to stop. Someone immediately recognises the owner of the voice; a little police inspector from Tarbes who shot a resistance fighter near Pau. He defends himself, he shouts that it's not true, it wasn't a resistance man but a thief, that it was in self-defence. I can sense the fear in his voice. It's dreadful to hear. Just to shut him up I'd like to join the others. We're too closely packed for me to wriggle through to them. But I'm ready to use my fists, I really want to use them, to put all the rage into them that I've been keeping inside myself for days. For once, rage is stronger than fatigue. My friend the pharmacy student has understood and holds me back.

In any case, it wouldn't do any good. Ladmiral and his group seem to have given up. I could almost weep.

Then everything is calm again. The silence is more frightening than the pushing and shoving just now. A leaden feeling in our heads, on our shoulders.

How much longer?

How long before we arrive?

How long until it's all over?

And how long until we get something to drink? The heat is becoming unbearable. Our tongues sticking in our mouths. Unless they're swollen enough to give the impression of being stuck to our palates. I touch my tongue. I use a little saliva to moisten my lips because my tongue can't. But it all dries straight away. No, not yet completely dry, there is sweat, a mixture of sweat and dirt which is solidifying, a paste on the skin like the bottom of a pond which hasn't quite dried up.

The train slows down again.

We're never going to get there!

I stretch up on tiptoe, levering myself on the shoulder of a comrade, trying to see something for I'm a long way from the opening. It's a small station with a long name. I just manage to read two letters: *V* and *i*. *V* and *i*, *Vi*. Not possible! *Vi*. Vie. Life—I don't know whether to laugh at what I've seen or whether it's a sign. Are we being mocked, we who are dying bit by bit? Or is it someone up there giving us a message?

Vie. Life.

There is life.

Live, don't die.

Not yet.

Anyway, the train doesn't stop.

No stop at *Vi*. Or no stopping life? Once again I start playing with words, as if that made any sense here. I know perfectly well it doesn't. That it never did. That it never will. The only thing that makes any sense is the water I want to drink. It's my body which is hurting, my back which can't hold out. And I've always been called tough in the face of suffering. Yes, I am tough in the face of suffering. Otherwise I would never have withstood the beatings, before the train. But the suffering is even tougher than me. I can feel that it's getting the upper hand. And I no longer have that arrogance, that lack of awareness that enabled me to bear the screaming of my torturers, their laughter, their sarcasm at my bloody nakedness. I am from now on without any defence. Now I have my trousers, but I'm in the process of losing my dignity.

Vi. Life.

All in all, I have to stick with those two letters, taunting me, and with that word: vie, life.

Yes, we've come past Vie-on-somewhere. I have to believe in it. I must believe in it.

I didn't see anything.

I didn't understand what was happening at all.

Suddenly hands were squeezing my neck, squeezing really hard, and I could hear noises like an animal howling. I saw the man, eyes bulging, howling, almost slavering and I heard the others around me shouting and the sounds of fighting, whilst I almost passed out in my turn. It was one of our group driven mad by the heat.

The comrades who were sitting have stood up. Three of them are holding him as best they can whilst two others are trying to lift me up to get my mouth closer to the skylight, like that comrade just now—when was that? I've seen this scene before. Was that me? Whilst I'm getting my breath back I can still hear the strangled cries of the other, as if he had wanted me to take on what was threatening him, as if he had tried to get rid of the horror inside himself by getting it out of me; and as if that horror was now rising in his own despairing throat. He's shaking, trembling uncontrollably and they can't even lay him down on the wagon's filthy straw. I close my eyes. First I hear a rattle in his throat and then nothing, though his body is still silently quivering. My eyes are still closed but I can see his body racked by spasms, and I see again the body of our comrade who was hanged at Riom, murdered by the pro-Nazi *Milice*[1] whilst we could do nothing, could try nothing. Those feet which went on jerking for a long time. Which still go on jerking in my head, and right down my back.

My God. Let this come to an end.

I don't know how much time has passed. I must have spent several minutes suspended between those feet in my memory and those which are hammering against the wagon floor. I don't even know how they finally managed to lay him down. When I open my eyes he's there, on the floor, taking up the space of four men. I don't know which I resent the more, that or the fit of madness which made him throw himself at me.

I'm feeling better.

I look at him.

He must be twice my age, but age is nothing here.

He's breathing with difficulty, panting, his lips are pale; saliva everywhere. But he is breathing. They've decided to leave him lying down. Some raise objections and tension mounts a notch once more. A bit of pushing and shoving throws two men onto the prostrate body of the unfortunate chap. A foot crushes his belly and another almost smashes his face. His nose and mouth are all bloody, his inner thigh soaked though I can't tell whether he's wet himself in his outburst, whether it's his pee or someone else's. But anyway, what difference does

_____
1 A force employed by the Vichy government of 1940-44 to re-press internal dissent (OED).

it make, how you wet or soil yourself? I hear myself asking this question, and I know I'm ridiculous. We're way beyond all that already, the words and the actions. And time goes on passing. I try to concentrate on the sound of the wheels turning. If only I could sleep a little.

I close my eyes.

I listen to the wheels.

I try to get rid of that sawing in my head, behind my eyes.

I try to dispel the images which keep coming back, as if they'd just been waiting for that to happen in order to reappear. My arrest at the Café de Paris, this 1 May. The dreadful fear when they surrounded me. The surprise I had to feign. The self-control I had which I never expected to have but had anyway. The composure as I showed my fake police ID card, explaining that I was one of Darnand's team, that I was there to eliminate a group of terrorists, that there was a perfectly simple explanation for the revolver on my belt and the bullet in the barrel.

When they showed me the address scribbled on a piece of paper found on the body of my friend Jean, my palms started sweating. I didn't want to take the paper. I pretended not to know him. And yet I did know him! I knew those lines which I'd written myself; they would easily have recognised the writing if they'd thought to make me write them again. Maybe they put that off for later, unsure, believing or pretending to believe the story I told with such self-assurance to the kind-looking man who was so much like me—as much in age as with the exhaustion showing in his face, suffusing his face.

From the Gestapo headquarters in the rue des Saussaies they sent me to Fresnes whilst they checked out my story. A few days' respite, or permanent salvation. I've never believed in salvation.

I'll never forget the sound of firing squads, almost every morning, in a courtyard behind the one my cell overlooked. I can still hear them in the wheels of the train. I'll still hear them until the end, until my last moment. Contrary to what I thought, the death of others is more agonising for me than my own. Because it is worse than my own death, which is only an idea, whereas in the death of others I am actually living my own death, now, I can see it, hear it, feel it in all its horror. Through their death I can see myself dying. Yes, what I remember of those days before Royallieu are those gunshots I could feel as if inside my own body every morning; I remember them more than I remember the fear of what was ahead for me, of what could not but be ahead for me because they would certainly discover what I was, even if not who I was. I still hear, still feel the cracks of those rifles, one after the other with my shoulders braced as if for the bullets. I feel them almost more than the beating I got the second time I was taken in front of that exhausted man, the man who seemed no more moved by the cries of my torturers than by those I tried to hold back, wanting to show off, not succeeding, then succeeding. I could almost have got on with him, and that was the worst, that's what comes back to me next, after the sound of the rifles, the similarity between us amidst the total, absolute, fundamental difference; and the feigned or genuine impassiveness we shared, me in my atrocious agony, he watching it. A detachment which seemed to bring us together beyond the flow of blood separating us. But it was my body jerking beneath the blows. Not his.

It was my blood.

Not his.

So no, we had nothing in common.

When they took me to Fresnes, I thought I'd be in the next batch for the firing squad, and was in such pain that I was glad of it. That I'd soon be amongst those comrades we heard going past in the early morning, sometimes at night, the lucky ones—or maybe the unluckiest?—who had embraced their wives for the last time in the visitors' room before being marched to the courtyard at the back. How could they have believed what I had finally tried to convince them of, that I was just a part-time agent of the Swiss Intelligence Service, born in Neuchâtel, sent first to Clermont then to Paris, with the only proof to back me up those documents they found in my apartment which didn't tell them much, revealed almost nothing.

But they had believed me. They'd believed me! Incredible. It made me almost angry to be fighting and not winning against an enemy who could be so stupid.

When they fetched me from my cell on 6 June, around midday, just when I thought all was over, I found myself in front of a doctor who wanted to check whether I was fit to be sent to Germany. To "travel"! He told me the Allies had landed. He said it almost with a smile, but perhaps I dreamt that. What a dreadful irony. I was being told that I wasn't going to die straight away, but that they were sending me to die further away, just when everything was coming to an end.

Another salvo sounds in my head.

I open my eyes.

It isn't in my head.

The train has stopped. There's a platform. Soldiers have been shooting at the skylight; one of the comrades was trying to pull the last slat away, one we'd not been able to shift earlier. Did they think we were going to try to escape through that ridiculous hole, covered in barbed wire, in full view of everyone?

Or did they just want to make sure that we would die of suffocation?

The bullets haven't hit anyone. The slat has come loose but is hanging off, held like the others by the tight mesh of barbed wire. A bit more air is getting in and, through the opening in the slats, we can see a bit better.

All is quiet. As if everyone is holding what little breath is left to him.

Then a few cries start in the wagon.

"Give us a drink!"

I'm dying of thirst too, and my head is spinning. Thinking about my cell in Fresnes almost made me forget all that. As if thinking was not without its use. In the end I don't know. What I do know is that my throat is burning and my head spinning with the thirst.

Someone says, "We're at Soissons. I recognise the station. It's my hometown."

His home. That sounds funny. It's a long time since I had somewhere to call home. Home, that could equally be this wagon, where we're about to die of thirst. They could give us something to drink. We've stopped. Why don't they give us a drink? I ask, "Why don't they give us a drink?" Several comrades take up the cry, "Yes! Give us a drink! Give us a drink!"

Through the slats I notice a man next to the shed facing us. He obviously wants to help us. But he isn't moving. He is there, but helpless; you'd think he's as desperate as we are, if that were possible.

I call out to him: "Why aren't they giving us anything to drink?"

He tries to reply, to make himself heard without shouting: "The Germans won't let us near. They're really angry. The resistance have blown up the tracks at Rheims and Châlons. They're getting their own back."

"But we're all going to die! It must be 40 degrees in here!"

"We've asked the Red Cross to step in. Hang on in there!"

Hang on in there. That's what he said. Hang on in there. But what is there to hang on to when you're as thirsty as I am, when you're suffocating in this oven, when you stink, when you don't know where you're going, when you no longer know where you are, who you are, when your stomach is aching and your back hurts enough to make you cry out loud. Good God, what is there to hang on to?

I'm thirsty. That's all I know. I'm thirsty. I'm thirsty. And I'll die if I don't get a drink. I'll die, and so will all those around me, all those calling out for a drink. The cries are all around. Cries of "Give us a drink" all around me. And when they can no longer call out, they're moaning. And I'm joining in with the cries outside and inside me. My body is nothing but thirst and cries, cries and thirst. Thirst. Thirst. I can't go on. I'm weeping. I've no more tears. I don't even have any tears left to drink. Nothing. It's appalling, what's happening to us. Can no one hear our cries? Is no one coming to help us?

And yet the man who is watching us so helplessly spoke of resistance. He said tracks have been blown up. So are there still people thinking of us, who don't want us to arrive at our destination, wherever that is—hell, no doubt?

But hell is right here. They should let us arrive. Anywhere would be better than here. Anywhere, nowhere, but not here beneath this murderous sun.

The man turns away from us and leaves the platform, his shoulders hunched.

He's going to find shade. He wants to disappear. Disappear into the shade and be forgotten. He disappears. But it's shade that we want. Shade, and water.

I've already forgotten his face. All we can think about is what he's going to do now, far from us, and about his freedom to be far from us, far from the train, far from the sun. Perhaps he's going to get a drink? Perhaps he's going to plunge into water? Perhaps there's a river in this village? Perhaps he's going to the river, this man who's left us in the blazing sun? Left us to die beneath this sun.

Cries are still filling the wagon. It seems no one has realised that shouting doesn't do any good, unless it's to speed death up perhaps? But that's just it, that's what they want. To die more quickly.

As if one of them has read my thoughts—and to say I'm still thinking, that I still have thoughts, is laughable—as if one of them has heard me, he succeeds in dying. His shout becomes strangled, then he suddenly goes quiet, his eyes open, his mouth open. And now there he is, a few metres away from me, leaning against the wall, his empty look towards me. Someone says, "He's dead." And the word goes around, "There's been a death."

Only one death? Does that mean the rest of us are alive?

We don't want to lay him down, where he'd take up space or be trodden on, so three comrades push up close to him to stop him falling. They'll take turns until someone comes to take the body away. But when will that be? And how long can they go on like this? They've closed his eyes and mouth. His face relaxes. I envy him. If he only knew how much I envy him. He collapses gently against the comrades, as if resting after all his suffering. And they prop him up until he collapses again. You'd think it was some sort of game. He collapses. They prop him up. He collapses. They prop him up. You could almost forget that he's dead. You could almost forget the weight of death on their shoulders.

Suddenly, someone says they've seen Red Cross nurses. He cries that we're going to be given something to drink, the body will be taken away, it's all coming to an end. There are the same cries all around. You can hear them from the next wagon. We'd forgotten that there were other wagons than ours, other cries than ours. The cries are growing louder, swelling, filling the whole train.

"Give us a drink!"

"Take the bodies away!"

"Give us a drink!"

"We're suffocating!"

"Give us a drink!"

As if the Germans didn't know we were close to death in here, suffocating, dying of thirst. As if the French on the platform didn't know it.

But nothing happens.

Suddenly the cries stop.

A detachment of soldiers is spreading out along the platform, their backs turned towards us.

We wait, on tenterhooks, not knowing what for. Hope returns, and that's more unbearable than anything. I've always thought that hope is what tortures you the most. I would never have expected to be so right. I would never have thought it could be so true, that hope is the sharpest, most precise torture, that it gets to you exactly at the point which makes the agony so intense.

For now the train is moving again, slowly. Preoccupied, no one notices at first. It gets underway without jolting, as if it wants to conceal from us that we're moving again, that the Red Cross can't do anything for us, that the nurses can't do anything for us, that they would not be allowed to come near us, that they would be prevented from helping us. Seeing the motionless soldiers moving, their backs turned towards us as if we didn't exist, we realise that we're the ones who are moving, that the train is off again and that there will be no help for us. We'll keep our dead comrade for ourselves, with us. He'll begin to properly decompose. To liquefy literally through his pores. And our throats will continue to get more parched. And our lungs to burn. Our whole bodies eaten up from the inside.

I look at the dead comrade that the others have managed to prop up, with his belt passed beneath his armpits, hanging from a nail or a hook behind. Now he stays up on his own, leaning slightly forward. He won't collapse again, we don't have to continue efforts to hold him up. He looks as if he's asleep, with his chin forward, as serious as anything.

I envy him, once again.

He's the lucky one, he's not thirsty any more.

His body will soon be dissolving, but he's no longer thirsty. His heart has stopped beating. He doesn't know how lucky he is not to feel his heart beating like mine, madly, faster, louder even than the wheels on the rails or in my head, my heart pounding enough to burst out of my chest, whilst my lungs struggle to inflate, struggle to fill with the small amount of air left to us. I can feel tingling in my fingertips, in my feet, as far as the roots of my hair. It reaches down to my chest, up to my belly. I feel as if I'm locked in a box, squashed in a vice, as if I'm myself the vice which is squashing me, as if my legs are pushing up into my belly and my shoulders into my chest. I want to loosen the vice. I want my lungs to dilate again, but no air comes in. I open my mouth and no air comes in. It's worse than in my worst nightmares when I cried out without a sound. I think I'm going to die like this, with my mouth open, saying nothing, with nothing coming out and nothing coming in.

But now the train is stopping again.

Are they going to leave us again to roast without moving? Has the line been blown up again? Do they not want us to arrive? There's pushing and shoving around the skylight without any consideration for others, without any thought for others—who could think of others? If we were not so crammed in I'm sure we'd be tearing each other apart by now.

But what we see outside holds us back, perhaps on the edge of doing the worst. Faces seem to come out of the woods. First, a woman. Then another, a child, a teenager. There must be others too, for the comrades at the other end of the train are calling to them.

"Give us a drink!"

Nothing happens, but we see the faces turning from one side to the other, as if seeking something.

Suddenly the woman holds a slate over her head. A school slate. Then the teenager does the same. It looks like a game. But no one wants to play. No one is inclined to laugh at this ridiculous ballet. I can't see what is written on the slate. Nor can the man next to me. Our vision is blurred by the heat, the thirst, the sweat. We try again. Then we seem to see "Saint Brice" written on the woman's slate, and on the child's "Rheims 4 km". To which we respond with a chorus of:

"Give us a drink!"

Again, the woman looks to right and left. She does not dare to come closer. But suddenly she gets a bucket out of the trees. She can't pass it to us, so she lifts it up and shows it to us as if to warn us about what she's going to do. Almost immediately my neighbour and I are splashed with water. It's unbelievable. It's unbelievably good. We stretch out our arms but the comrades behind us grab us. They want their share. And we hadn't even opened our mouths, we weren't prepared. We spend our time with our mouths open to breathe the scorching air and we didn't even manage to keep them open for those few drops of water which might be our salvation. The whole wagon is in an uproar. It could turn nasty, but as usual we hear that voice trying to calm things down:

"Calm down! They've got more. Take it in turns."

Almost no one hears. And the nice order we were in when we left is overturned. As I try to edge away to avoid the violence I nearly fall under the feet. I finish up at the other end, at the side overlooking the tracks. But evidently the woman is not alone for other heads have appeared on this side too. Local people seem to be everywhere. So have they understood what was happening to us?

Water splashes sporadically.

Suddenly something bangs into the skylight on the side where I am now. I can't believe my eyes. It's a carrot they've thrown us which is caught on the barbed wire. I would have preferred a juicy fruit, something moist, but it's better than nothing. I haven't yet eaten the lump of dubious sausage meat they gave us at Compiègne, which I've kept rolled in a handkerchief in my trouser pocket; I'm fearful that eating it will be worse than anything in this heat where even the living themselves are rotting and high. So a carrot is always good to have. I reach out with my hand, my arm, I stretch as far as I can, I'm up on tiptoe, my whole body stretching out to grab this ridiculous carrot dangling from its wire, defying me. I curse my short stature, although it's been useful to me in the past. I'd like to be twice my height to get to this wretched vegetable. Suddenly the little saliva I have left floods into my mouth. I can already taste the sweetness, maybe there's some juice after all. A carrot must have some water in it. My fingers are almost there, I can touch it, but then a hand pushes my hand away, an arm shoves against mine. A shoulder pushes me sideways. It's one of the others trying to get it for himself. And here we are like a couple of kids fighting to pinch a pot of jam. He's taller than me. He's going to make it, and I'll get nothing. The bastard! A wave of anger like that of a child comes over me.

But the train sets off again, suddenly, and the carrot comes loose and falls onto the track. He's not going to get it any more than I am.

I'm glad. To my shame.

I'm glad.

If only he hadn't pushed me. I would have given him some of it. Or perhaps not.

It's shameful. I'm glad he didn't get it. That he wasn't any more successful in reaching it than I was. That he didn't taste it in his mouth any more than I did.

We look at each other, hatred in our eyes. Then, defeated, we drop back.

Those few drops of water were not enough. It's worse than before. Why did they throw us those bottles, those vegetables we couldn't catch? You'd think the Germans had summoned them to make the torture even worse. I remember Tantalus. So that wasn't a myth, a story for children, a lesson for schoolboys. It exists, it's real. It's true you can do that to a man, put the end of his suffering at his fingertips and then snatch it away, show him water, grab the bread from his mouth, just to hear him wail more loudly.

I wail silently.

But the train is stopping again. We haven't even gone a kilometre since we lost the carrot. What's he doing up there at the front, him in the engine? Has he too been ordered to torture us? Are they all at it?

We can see the end of a platform and market gardens at the edge of the tracks. Have they really got vegetables here? Are they not starving like the Parisians?

Once again there are men on the tracks. Some are carrying baskets. We can see all sorts of colours in the baskets, overflowing with green, red and orange. I'd almost forgotten such colours existed. Out in the sun they would almost hurt your eyes.

I pray with all my might for them to come closer, even if it's really water I want. I pray they'll give us everything they've got in their baskets, all that life they're carrying that our bodies are crying out for, desperate for.

But a stone just misses one of the men. And then almost immediately a shot rings out. It seems a soldier has fired in the air. The men with the baskets stop short. As if the whole thing had been prearranged, their careful approach, their baskets, the colours in their baskets, the slow movement of all those colours, the stone, the shot, their coming to a halt. As if they were putting on a show for us. As if we were the stupefied spectators at some hellish pageant.

Then the train sets off again, very slowly.

Then stops.

We're no longer advancing more than a few metres at a time. What are they up to, at the front?

At the side of the tracks there are more and more people, men, women, a few children. They're not saying anything. They're not moving. They're looking at us. We're looking at them too. That's all that's left for us to do, to look at each other. But the soldiers come back and get between them and us. They must be on both sides. We start calling out again, begging for a little water. But no one moves. They're as if paralysed. And yet, there seems to be some movement behind them. Some of them turn their heads towards the gardens. Others keep looking at us. I don't know what's happening. It doesn't make much sense, for us to be calling out whilst they keep quiet and turn their heads. But someone in the wagon says, "They've got a hose!"

It seems to be true. A gardener is pointing his hose towards us. Will he dare to turn it on? We pile upon one another. On the other side they must not have anything, for they're all trying to get to our side. We'll be crushed to death.

"Wait! Wait till he turns the hose on. We must get organised. Get your shirts. Take turns at the skylight."

We're shoving each other out of the way; we try to obey but the thirst is too great. And the man is still not doing anything. He seems to be hesitating.

But now he's turning on the tap and aiming the hose at our wagon. We expect to hear a rifle shot. But nothing happens. So we open our mouths, we hold out our shirts, we jostle but manage to take turns. The man directs the hose from one skylight to the other. Some of it gets into the wagon. Our shirts are wet. Too bad if it's dirty, too bad if it makes us ill, it's water, water, it's water. We don't want it to stop. It stops. He's watering the wagon in front. We'd rather the others were dead, that we were the only ones left, in our wagon, that our wagon was the only one left, that all the water was for us. The water comes back. He's watering us again. It's wonderful, wonderful. But it stops too soon. He's watering the wagon behind. Then the cries grow louder, like the cries of children. All these serious people in this wagon, these men, some of them warriors, crying out like children.

"Our turn! Our turn!"

When the water comes back there's more jostling, a sort of panic, a mixture of joy and anguish.

An oasis in the desert, too small for all these men, from now on I know what an oasis is. What it can mean for a man in the desert. Our wagon, like a caravan lost beneath the blazing sun. This water saving us, like the manna of our forefathers. And words come back to me, whilst the water splashes us. I tell myself I'm still alive. That if words can still come to me then I'm not completely dead. Then the water leaves us again, goes to sprinkle the next wagon. And then comes back again.

I don't know how long this goes on, but it's amazing it can happen. We don't know why the soldiers allow it. But they do allow it.

We've managed to soak our shirts with all this water, thinking that we'll be able to suck a few more drops from the sodden material; and whilst the train slowly sets off again a few of us have the courage to shout thanks to the man who has given us renewed hope.

For we have foolishly begun again to believe that we can get out of this. We've begun to imagine that the worst is over, that things will get better.

We believe it as the train moves forward, even if the scorching air coming in is roasting us slowly as it makes contact with the water on our skin. Blisters are forming underneath my feet and the feet of the others. The mixture of sweat and condensation, and friction with the equally hot floor, continually increases our suffering. One of our number, desperate, has removed his trousers and his underwear. One by one we do the same. Some, and I'm one of them, at least keep our underpants on, not out of modesty but to avoid having our buttocks scraping against the wood. Very soon many are stark naked, trampling underfoot their clothes drenched in sweat and stagnant water. The mad euphoria of a few minutes ago, when the water was splashing down, has given way to apathetic misery; I can't even raise a smile at the grotesque sight of our poor denuded bodies, our ever more pitiful genitals, our hideous bellies, our worn-out legs. I think, if they wanted to turn us into cattle they've now succeeded. Now we're closest to what they wanted us to look like. Our last vestiges of dignity disappeared when the water splashed onto us.

We can no longer manage to stand and sit in order. We do it haphazardly as if nothing, nobody is guiding us any longer.

I look for Ladmiral, but I can't make him out amongst this confused mass we've become now. Our faces, our bodies, don't resemble anything; or rather, they resemble each other in their nothingness. We are all becoming the same. We're all one, an unrecognisable heap. Everything we were, what made us individuals, our distinctive faces—all that is beginning to fade away.

But now the train is stopping again.

We listen. We try to understand what's happening. We try to detect the slightest sign of hope, the slightest chance of our faces being human again. Nothing happens. Until the train reverses.

We don't understand anything.

We don't dare to hope.

We're right not to dare. Not to hope.

The train stops. We wait.

In the silence of the wagon I realise that everyone's stopped talking. With the noise of the wheels I hadn't been paying attention, but it must have been for quite a time already, probably since Saint Brice.

Probably because it's been getting hotter and hotter since then, the heat more and more stupefying, literally stunning us. Those who are able to stick close to the skylights or the cracks in the door can get a little air from outside. The others, and I am one of them, being now too far away, try not to move. My back, my hands, all my limbs, are scorching hot.

It can't be any later than three o'clock in the afternoon. You'd think the sun had stopped in its tracks, immobilised like us in this furnace, as if everything has come to a halt, determined to keep us trapped in this furnace. And we're burning inside as well as outside. I wonder whether it's more intolerable since we were sprinkled with the hose. The moist air is worse than what we'd been breathing since this morning. My throat is on fire as if with alcohol I haven't swallowed properly; each breath brings on a sharp stab in my lungs, forcing me to cry out and I'm not sure it's a silent cry.

I notice that the latest jostling has landed me next to the pharmacy student from earlier. I don't think he's recognised me in the blinding heat. I don't make any gesture to him. I hardly have the strength and I don't want to waste what energy I have left to try to resist this internal burning. I save up my movements as I would any water I might be given. But I'm no longer even thinking about water. I only think about this foul air which I wish I didn't have to breathe, which I wish I could breathe in deeply. It seems as if we've been in the wagon for days, days we've been stopped beneath this brutal sun.

Soon my head is swimming, and all around me there's movement, swarming, like an ocean of swarming insects, a frightening swarm; silence gives way gradually to a vague buzzing which invades my head. I don't know if it's inside me or if it comes from this mass tightening around me, pinning me. Trapping me inside myself.

And I close my eyes.

I tell myself I shouldn't close my eyes, I hear myself saying, "Don't close your eyes", but my eyelids are heavy, my head even heavier. I try not to move, to concentrate on my own immobility and the train's; I try to stop the buzzing around me, to get past my closed eyelids to stop the buzzing, the swarming in my ears.

It is the dull sound of moaning coming off all these bodies, off my own body. I don't know who is moaning, whether it's all those around me or me myself, my burning lungs or this wagon where I'm going to die. For I know now that I'm going to die here, that I'll burn alive here, from the inside out. It cuts through me. The image of my burnt body cuts through me, I can see my skin coming away, inside, the inside of my mouth feels raw.

I open my eyes, woken suddenly by the disgusting sound of a body emptying itself. I don't know whether it's the man who died earlier, if it's me or one of the others. But a body has suddenly emptied and brought me back to life. The stink just as much as the sound has aroused me from that deadly torpor. The stink of that emptied body, the stink of our rotting bodies, inside as well as outside, of our bodies steeped in our own filth.

Someone cries out:

"Air! Open the door! For pity's sake, open the door!"

It's my neighbour. It's as if the horrendous smell, the disgusting sound, has roused him, like me, from the slow slide towards oblivion.

The voice becomes more precise, knowledgeable, explaining: "It's the straw fermenting, and the sweat evaporating. We shouldn't have taken our clothes off. It produces carbon dioxide. And urine makes ammonia. We're being poisoned."

Then, as if that was all they'd been waiting for to rouse them, as if they'd suddenly been made aware of their situation by these words announcing their absurd, abject death beneath the blazing sun, everyone starts shouting, banging on the walls with their feet, with their fists, some with their heads, calling for the door to be opened, for air, not to be left to die like animals, that even animals wouldn't be treated like this. They shout, they bang on the walls, they howl. Feet are howling as well as heads. You'd think we were in a lunatic asylum, and no doubt we are all mad now, and I'm as mad as they are, shouting and howling with them, when I'd promised myself to stay still, not to waste the small amount of strength I had left. I'm probably shouting louder than any of them. Nobody can stop us now. Nothing can stop us howling, though we're on the verge of passing out. Even Ladmiral must be shouting with us. The lack of water was dreadful this morning; now it's really appalling, worse than anything we've experienced so far, as if they're trying out all sorts of death on us. And we bang on the walls, we'll die more quickly by banging, by howling.

I hear a comrade near the skylight shouting to someone he's seen, someone who must be looking unbelievingly at this train full of the sound of howling, someone who must not be able to believe his ears; the comrade shouts to him to go and fetch help, to get us out of here. But the only response is a violent banging on the door. We're still calling out. We're yelling for the door to be opened, for some air to be let in. Another bang shakes the door, then several more. It's the banging of rifle butts. But we keep on yelling, nothing will stop us calling out. As if that was all that was left for us to do, to call out, and for those not calling, huddled and breathless, then passing out, to die amongst the cries.

For I can see that for some, crying out has finished them off, as if crying out was all they had been waiting for to die. One of them, behind me, is doubled over; I turn to support him, to raise his head, but I can see his pupils are dilated, two ghastly holes where his eyes had been, and another gaping hole, his mouth, distorted and never to close again. I let him drop. I can't do anything for him, and I go back to crying out with the others. I see the man next to the skylight taking hold of the barbed wire with both hands as if he couldn't feel anything and trying to drag it away, the blood running down over his wrists and then his arms. He shakes the wire violently, bangs on the loose slat which the wire is still holding in place, when suddenly a rifle shot rings out, then another.

Then everything stops. Then we stop crying out.

I didn't think it possible, but here we are, silent again. Surprise stopped us in mid-cry. And it's surprise I see in the eyes of the comrade at the skylight, as if he hasn't realised what is happening to him, as if he hasn't felt the bullet piercing his forehead, passing into his head just above his eye. For a moment he remains upright, his hands clenched around the barbed wire, soaked in blood which is also slowly running down his forehead. And when he collapses, the remains of his hands are shredded on the barbed wire netting.

Behind the netting a voice breaks into the dreadful silence which has spread amongst us:

"Ruhe, deine Maule! Ruhe, Schweinhund!"

Well, he won't be saying anything now, that's for sure. And we won't either, as if the whole wagon has been thunderstruck. We've been asking for air, and they've shot at us. We'd asked them for air, as if we'd forgotten who they are, as if we'd forgotten that they'd shut us in here, suffocating amidst these lethal fumes at temperatures of 50, 60, perhaps 70 degrees. And it was from them that we were asking for help. With them that we were pleading. Them. And help, they've given it. They've given it to the comrade who fell by the skylight, and whose body we're dragging with difficulty towards the middle of the wagon, in order to take his place near the opening. If I'd still had the strength I myself would have slipped in there, would have taken his place, perhaps using my fists to get through. But I've sat down again, like some of the others, like almost all the others. The silence has never weighed so heavily, laden with all our cries, all those cries to which the only response was a bullet in a man's head, all those cries to which the only response is this exhausted silence.

For everyone seems exhausted, except three or four who, realising that the door will never open, suddenly pull out blades which had escaped the searches. They are frantically trying to widen the holes in the wood, some of them in the floor, others in the walls of the wagon, as if they want to escape even though they no longer have the strength. Yet there's no one any longer to stop them. As if the thought of being shot no longer bothered anyone, as if that were no longer important, as if the man lying a few metres away with a hole in his head were an object of envy, like the other still hanging from his belt, or like all those we're walking over now without even realising it.

In any case, those who haven't passed out don't have the strength to protest, nor the strength to hack at the wood.

I don't myself have either a knife or a piece of metal, but I start mechanically rubbing at the wall with my mess tin. I realise it's useless but I stick to it. It's better than letting yourself go without doing anything.

I rub away slowly, not having the strength to do more.

I rub, the lip of the tin is wearing down but the wood stays solid.

I rub without hope, for the sake of rubbing.

I've scarcely dislodged a few splinters. At this rate, I'll be dead before I've rubbed away a millimetre. But that doesn't bother me. I've found something to do to keep me going a while longer, that's all, to do as those who're still battling on, pretending they believe in it. I stick to my tin without thinking about anything anymore, without trying to think. It's not me rubbing at the wood, it's someone who once was me, who once bore my name, who once bore a different name from the one I have at present, someone whose sole purpose in life now is to rub the wood slowly, almost meticulously. I don't even know any longer why I'm rubbing. If I remembered that it was to make a hole I think I would go mad at the thought of the time that would take. I concentrate on the wood I'm rubbing and I rub without knowing why I'm rubbing.

I don't know how long my hand has been moving back and forth like this, gripping the metal, already cramping up and contracting in spasms—is it because of the effort?

Perhaps it's just started?

Or perhaps it's been for hours?

But if it had been for hours, I would be dead. I would have been dead for a long time.

That's the only way I know it can't have been for hours.

So perhaps I've only been here, rubbing, for a few seconds?

Or has my hand been coming and going like this, almost in a vacuum, for a few minutes?

Ten?

Fifteen?

What I do know is that the nearest comrade with a knife has managed to make a hole by separating two of the floor planks. Straight away he fixes his mouth to the hole, as if he can't see the filth around him. He stays like this for a long time, his face against the floor, breathing deeply, not knowing what he's breathing in. When he gets up he sees me looking at him, my face drawn, not moving, the mess tin almost squashed in my hands. Then he hands me his knife and sticks his head back down to the floor. Praying to which God?

And now the blade he passed to me is forcing itself between the planks in its turn, pushing them slightly apart, setting about the wood to make the hole bigger. Its point attacks the edges, widens the gap. A slight turn of the wrist detaches a wood chip and brings it up to the surface. Another turn. And another one.

I'm getting the hang of this.

My hand moving steadily finds a rhythm, slow but precise.

I concentrate on the movement of my hand.

I am that hand.

I'm my hand, digging.

I'm in its movement, I am its movement. I can't do anything different, otherwise I'll die.

And with concentration, an image comes to me, and I cling to it as if I'll live and die by images as much as I did by words in the past. I don't see anything around me anymore except the movement of my hand, and with that movement a story other than mine, another image. I don't see the dead bodies piling up, with their heads hanging down on their chests, or lying around our feet, under our feet. I don't see the man with a bleeding nose under my feet, I don't see anything, or if I see him I put him into that other image that I've conjured up to keep me going. It's ridiculous but I see, more clearly than anything around me, Edmond Dantès expiring in his dungeon. I'm the unlucky one who'll manage to get away, to take revenge, taking the place of the dead man, all the dead men, around me.

And I dig away methodically, as if I had a goal, beyond that little breath of air that I need, that little breath of air which I absolutely have to have if I'm to hang on a little longer. I don't want to think about anything else. I close my eyes whilst I dig, I'm still inside the movement of my hand, completely inside it, the turning of my wrist, the mechanical quarter-turn which brings up the wood chips, in this growing hole, in this miraculous knife which is carving out a little air for my mouth, a thin stream I take in, a tiny amount which is going to save me; I can feel that it will save me. I'm this thin stream of air invading my body, which will get me out of this prison.

I come to a little and notice that the train has set off again because the air current has strengthened.

And just as I begin to breathe more normally, just as I have the impression that I'm climbing out of the abyss into which I'd begun inexorably sliding, a hand grabs my shoulder and throws me violently backwards. Who can still have such strength?

I don't understand what's happening to me.

Thrown backwards, I stumble over another body behind me; I scarcely have time to realise what's happening when another is on top of me, then another falling onto my back.

A fight has started, a savage fight, and I don't know why. Over a place near a hole? For a breath of air? Out of sheer madness?

Very quickly, there's an unbelievable scrum.

Terrifying.

Indecent.

I try with all my strength to shift these bodies off my back, these bodies which are crushing me but protecting me at the same time. I can see comrades charging at one another. Some use the knives or pieces of glass in their hands to tear at the faces of those opposite them. Others are defending themselves or attacking with their mess tins, or their shoes, or their fists. Another has grabbed a belt and to clear himself a space is whirling it round as widely as he can. I can hear the dull sound of the buckle hitting their heads, I can hear the cries of pain, the shouts of rage, the inhuman cries of animals. These are no longer men who are shouting.

I see another man throttling everyone he sees, the living and the dead, the dead bodies and the dying.

I'm still trying to extricate myself and get away from the carnage, but my leg is caught beneath a heap of tangled arms, legs, heads. A hand is holding onto my ankle. I kick out to make it let go. I feel my naked foot striking soft flesh, piercing the flesh.

The hand doesn't let go, it tightens, more and more like a dead man's hand. But a dead man wouldn't have such strength.

I kick out again, I try to turn around to use my fists in my turn.

Trying to get up I see a comrade disembowelling another with a shard of glass. I close my eyes to shut it out, so as not to see those hands rooting around in the guts, those hands covered in red and black fluid, so as not to see the madness around me and which I feel mounting inside myself.

I close my eyes, and my leg goes on kicking to disentangle itself. It kicks out. Kicks. Kicks. Soon it's kicking against emptiness, but still kicking.

I can hear cries from all around at once, beside me, above me, below me, inside me. All the fury which earlier we put into yelling and banging on the wood we're now turning upon ourselves. Those who only a few hours ago were helping each other are now setting about each other. I would like to get out of the scrum, get to the other end of the wagon where I've seen some men huddled, and push away those who've been overtaken by madness. But I have time to see some bodies extricating themselves even from there to go and kill or be killed in that indescribable crush.

I call for help.

I gulp.

I beg to be taken out of here.

I cry out.

I can't hear anything anymore.

I can't hear myself crying out.

I'm nothing but the jerking of my leg, the loosening of my fists.

Someone hits me. I pass out.

When I come to the fight is still going on, but a metre away from me, and my leg is free. Someone has got me out of there.

I can see comrades pulling corpses out of the scrum, piling them up to make a sort of wall between us and those who are still killing each other. I understand that the only thing to do is to prevent contact between them and us, to keep them away until they're done for, disembowelled, strangled, faces smashed, limbs broken. We have to keep that madness away from us until it's run its course. We have to put the dead between it and ourselves if we don't want to finish up like them.

My back and ankle are hideously painful, my body covered in burning cuts, but I manage to get up and help those who've pulled me out of that lunacy, to do like them, to drag myself along to pile up lifeless bodies, to barricade ourselves behind bodies. I recognise the young pharmacy student as I drag him towards the heap. He's missing an eye. In its place there's just a monstrous red hole. No teeth left in his mouth. But I don't have time to think about him. I hoist him onto the heap.

I try to fetch another, but I collapse. All I hear are the noises getting fainter, the cries getting less frequent, the rate of blows slowing down. I don't know if it's in my head or the wagon.

Finally the noise of the train takes over.

I pass out again.

I wake up. The train has stopped again. A comrade is wiping my face with a damp rag. Moans are coming from all around, from the heap of bodies in the middle of the wagon, from the corners where the wounded have been dragged. The comrade says, "Not too good eh? But you'll see, we're going to get more air. And then night is coming."

I don't reply.

I look around me.

I understand why there'll be more air.

In the other half of the wagon there are easily thirty or fifty dead bodies, in a pile, a gruesome heap. Fifty comrades fewer to be breathing. But breathing what? The stink is infernal.

Tough, it still means there's more space. At last I can stretch out, not think about anything anymore, not think at all. I slide down onto the damp straw.

But the same person—or another—picks me up and sits me down against the wall. "You mustn't drop off to sleep straight away." He slides a lump of sugar into my mouth. It's true, we had some sugar before we left. And bread. Even the putrid sausage they gave us at Compiègne. No water, but I can tell that from my mouth. In the fight everything's been crushed, mixed in with that filthy pulp of our soaking clothes, the blood and the flesh of our comrades. How has he managed to hang on to this sugar? And how can he give it to me? I thank him with a look. The lump is stuck to my tongue, between my swollen tongue and my palate. The sweetness makes me salivate horribly, but I don't have the strength anymore to be thirsty. It's burning my throat. I tell myself it's good. That it has to be good.

I'm exhausted, but I can feel there's still movement around me. They're dragging bodies, sorting the corpses, separating those still moving from those already stiff. The heap is almost up to the ceiling; it's wide enough at the bottom to stop it collapsing. Let's hope it will withstand the jolting of the train.

Someone says, "Let's do the count." Straight away the voices start up, ominous, sorrowful, counting as they did at school.

"One."

"Two."

"Three."

When my turn comes I say, "Thirty-six." I didn't think there were still so many of us. And it goes on after me, up to fifty-nine. I notice that Ladmiral is not amongst them, he must be in the heap. Three severely injured comrades are in too bad a way to respond. Those near to them count for them, without being sure that they're not speaking for dead men. A fourth has lost his mind, raging, foaming at the mouth. They've had to tie up his arms and legs with belts. His efforts to free himself have exhausted him, but he's still struggling, painfully. Someone says for him, "Sixty-three."

So there are sixty-three of us.

Sixty-three left.

Sixty-three who've escaped that nightmare.

Sixty-three out of the hundred at the start.

Sixty-three who've survived, but for how long?

Tears are running down my face. I didn't know I was still capable of crying. The comrade who's been taking care of me has noticed and is talking to me gently. I don't understand what he's saying but I like him talking to me. I no longer know if I'm crying about what I've seen, about all these deaths, about Ladmiral, or because he's talking to me, so gently, because he still has the strength to talk to me so gently. The presence of my brothers could not do me more good than that of this stranger talking to me.

A discussion starts up close to me. Someone says we should ask the Germans to get the corpses out. They say we can't keep them like this. That the stink is unbearable. That even the Germans must be able to smell it, that it must be unbearable for them too, that that's obvious. But I very soon hear them give up the idea. That if they didn't open up before, they're not going to open up now. That they'll never open up. That we'll never get out of this hell. That this is where hell is, not anywhere else, and that this is where they wanted to bring us.

We still don't understand.

We don't understand what has happened.

We don't understand this unrelenting harshness. Why they're doing it to us. We don't understand anything.

Then, after a time, they stop talking, stop trying to understand.

They stop asking why. Seeking the meaning of it.

We just stare at the bodies, the dark mass of them at the end of the wagon.

We can see stiff arms, legs broken in two, smashed noses, ears torn off, mouths agape. It's not true that a dead person becomes peaceful. Not these dead in any case. Our dead are hideous. Their faces purple beneath the dried blood, their lips blackened, their bellies so swollen that we expect to see them explode at any moment, to give way beneath the pressure of the gases filling them.

But the stink is already so bad, it wouldn't make much difference.

Instinctively we hold what remains of our clothes to our noses.

Two comrades take it upon themselves to cover the bodies with straw, as much to hide them from view as to soak up everything trickling from the heap, oozing and sometimes running out in thick, sticky smears.

I've put a shirt over my head and I'm breathing through it, not seeing anything. But nothing can stop me hearing the gurgling coming from the shapeless mass. You can hide your eyes, block your nose, but our ears give us away. You can't do anything about them, you can't trick them. They betray us. Through them, the dead continue talking to us, moaning in their own language, a sort of dull, sepulchral, obstinate bubbling.

I can't not hear them. Only the sound of the train on the move again would release me.

But the train is obstinately refusing to move; it is determined to keep us captives of this furnace, of the filthy stink and sounds; it forces us to listen to all the seething, these sounds of putrefaction which won't leave us in peace.

Perhaps that's why someone starts speaking again. He suggests we should pray for the dead.

Pray?

Who could still want to pray?

Who could still believe in something? In someone?

We pray. We pray out loud. We pray loudly. I'm almost yelling the phrases which I forced myself to learn, not so long ago. Others' words that I made my own so as not to give myself away. "Our Father . . ."

Our Father who art in heaven, not on the earth.

Our Father who art everywhere, but not in this wagon.

Our Father who art not my father, and certainly not the father of all these dead men who are singing thy praises in their own way, that squelchy gurgling.

I recite the Lord's Prayer with my comrades.

And I realise it's doing me good.

I'm seeking different words, not too unfamiliar, pursuing words which can help me further, and I gradually fall asleep, my lips stop moving, my dry mouth can hardly open, my voice fades away.

✳

And now I'm next to a stream, and not even surprised. It's rushing along at my feet. There's another one behind me. And another. They're all around me. I'm thirsty.

I'm hot. I'd like to dive in, let all this water run over me, but my feet are caught in the clay, I can't move. It's not running water, it's a marsh. I'm walking in a marsh which stretches into the distance. The earth is swallowing me up. When I pull my leg up it makes a sucking sound. My ankle is burning dreadfully. I pull one foot out of the mud. I put it down a bit further on. It sinks in, sending gurgling bubbles up to the surface. My foot sticks, I pull, it doesn't come. I pull again, pain shoots through my whole body. I pull, it doesn't come. I manage to pull myself out of the mud. There's nothing on the end of my leg. My foot has gone.

I wake up. I think I cried out.

The train is moving on in the darkness.

A small amount of air is coming in through all the holes we made, through the gaps we created with knives. The stink is unbearable, but air is circulating. In the other half of the wagon I can see the black mass swaying to and fro with the jolting of the train, like a great heap of jelly, to the right, to the left. It holds up. You'd say that all those bodies have become one huge, monstrous body in the darkness.

My ankle is hurting. I pass my slimy hand over it. I rub it with my oozing palm. A balm of my own sweat, sweetness from this filth seeping out of me.

Opposite me a sleeping comrade is delirious, as I must have been no doubt. He's talking about his wife, his children. I don't understand it all. Words get lost in his mouth. I crawl up to him and put my hand on his forehead. He's boiling hot. I turn his head towards the wall, I try to push his face towards a small crack where the air is coming in. It's all I can do for him. I go back to my corner.

The comrade next to me has seen me moving, he asks if I'm OK. Yes, I tell him. I tell him I'm OK. He knows as I do what that means: I'm OK; I'm alive; I'm still half alive. I ask if he's OK too. He says yes.

Then, in this foetid darkness, through the rags covering our noses, our mouths, we start to talk, in whispers, as if we mustn't wake those rotting away beside us.

He must be older than me, but it's impossible to guess his age exactly. I look at him. His eyes are distended with fever and fatigue, his cheeks swollen with the skin coming away in places. I think I must look like that, that I'm like him, that we all have the same ravaged faces and the same age now. He tells me he's from Paris, the fifteenth arrondissement like me, but from the Balard area. We swap a few familiar names: Boucicaut, Lourmel, Cambronne, Convention, Javel, Emile Zola, La Motte-Picquet Grenelle. So wonderful, all these names. It's amazing how beautiful they are, how lovely they sound, suddenly reappearing from a faraway past, impossible, almost incomprehensible hearing them in this wagon. And yet, two months ago, I was still wandering around these streets, crossing these squares, without any idea that there was anything extraordinary about their names.

He tells me he ran a bistro in the rue Leblanc and that in 1943 an American air raid nearly killed him, him and his clients. I tell him I remember that air raid. That I knew a girl who died in it, the newsagent. Decapitated by an iron shard. As I say that I think I shouldn't have,

I was wrong to speak about it, that it will bring us back to the horror we're in, but my neighbour doesn't seem to notice, he goes on talking. He talks about life in the bistro. About his clients. About those who grumbled all the time, not only since the war started, or those who on the other hand knew how to make him laugh. He says, "And yet I'm not a cheerful chap." The phrase comes up a few times. I'm not a cheerful chap. And I wonder whether I'm one, if I was one, if I could ever be one. He tells me he lost his wife very young and has never got over it. That he's never remarried. Girls a few times, just for the pleasure. Because he misses it too much. He speaks without shame. In a low voice he gives me a few details which embarrass me, and I resent him for it. I can't help thinking that it's such a cliché, two men in the darkness talking about women, it's almost laughable. Especially here. But he continues, forcing me perhaps to share his straightforwardness. Not to feel superior. To leave all that behind too, the past, the knowledge which places you above others, the abject foolishness of knowledge. To be a man here too, listening to another man talking about women amongst the corpses. So I listen to him, sometimes responding, and our words move forward like this, in the dark and the stink, almost making us forget the unbearable smell, the oozing heap of bodies at our feet:

"So are you married?"

"No. Too young."

"Got a girlfriend?"

"No."

"Never had a woman?"

"No."

"So you'll die a virgin."

He says it just like that, not maliciously, rather something sadly self-evident. Without knowing why, I can't help replying almost sharply: "No, I'm not going to die." It's what comes to me at this precise moment. A sort of idiotic pride. Totally unthinking. Miraculous.

Almost immediately I regret this undue optimism.

But, without saying anything, he has understood. This man, whom I was ready to despise a moment ago, who was talking to me about girls as if he was behind his bar on the Place Balard and I was standing with a drink in my hand, this man simply puts his hand on my arm without a word. I thank him in the same way, silently. Despite the squalid contact of our filth-covered bodies I feel that I've perhaps never been so close to anyone as at that precise moment.

We don't go on talking. We have no need to talk now.

Silence and fatigue soothe us.

Soon we're dozing, then we fall asleep.

We're woken by the sound of a few drops dripping from the roof; it's some light rain which is finally falling. I lost my mess tin in the brawl but I remember seeing in a corner the food tin which we were using at first as a mobile chamber pot; we haven't used it for a long time now, we've made do with one end of the wagon, near the heap of bodies. They've left us enough space for this luxury, almost a proper toilet, over to one side, where we can't be seen except perhaps by the wide-open eyes of those providing our screen . . . So I get down on all fours, feeling for the tin so that I can collect some water in it. I move forward in the dark, now and then catching a foot or a leg, sometimes the face of someone muttering, lying asleep or dying, sometimes the upright leg of someone still managing to stand up to breathe.

After a few minutes of this strange manoeuvre, amongst all these bodies, I finally put my hand on the tin, where I remembered seeing it, where my subconscious memory had placed it, like a glorious trophy that I had to dig up and which I'm now digging up in the darkness of the wagon. I clean it up as best I can with a rag and a bit of straw. I tell myself that we're so far beyond being disgusted that it doesn't matter. Our guts and our souls have experienced worse, since five o'clock this morning—I can scarcely believe that it's not even a day since we left Royallieu.

Once the tin is "cleaned" I get up and collect a few drops, searching for the biggest hole, the largest gap between the planks of the roof. The drips are slimy, thick, no doubt full of coal dust. But it's still water. And I don't dare stretch my arm out through the skylight for fear of the guards' rifle shots. I realise I'm back to caring about my own skin.

As there's very little rain and the speed of the train is pushing it to the sides, it takes forever to fill the bottom of the tin. Someone takes over and I turn around to sit down.

I've lost my place next to the comrade from just now.

It almost makes me weep.

I realise I haven't even asked his name. We've spoken about Paris and the places we loved, we've listed the names of places, but our own names, no, not mentioned. As if we no longer have names. True, mine is a false name anyway. But still, it's my name here.

I slide between two bodies lolling against the wall. The one on the left is boiling hot. He has a fever, but he isn't moving. The one on the right has a hat clamped over his face. I realise he's protecting himself from the smell and I envy him for having managed to keep such an accessory intact despite the brawl. Before the war I never liked hats, but this one seems to me very useful. But I realise very quickly that the body on the right is as cold as the one on the left is hot.

So I knock the hat off.

I can make out his face in the darkness. His cheeks are swollen. His mouth is open and the piece of bread he has stuffed into it to asphyxiate himself is sticking out through his bloated lips. I feel sick, and at the same time I admire someone who has been able to do that, who has had the strength to do it, to kill himself like that, not to fight back against the convulsions, the spasms of his body.

I put the hat back over his face and call for someone to help me drag him to the other side. We lift him under the arms. His body remains folded. We leave him at the foot of the heap, as if he were sleeping sitting up, with his hat over his face. At peace behind his hat.

Whilst this has been going on the food tin has filled up a little. We all want to rush for it. A tall chap who frightens us a bit says that first we're going to give some to the wounded. I thank him inwardly for taking over. He's protecting us from ourselves. Straight away I help to get the tin passed to the four who're in the worst state. When our turn comes there's virtually nothing left. I take the tin again to try to catch a little more water, but the rain has clearly stopped. I regret not having had the courage to stretch my hand through the skylight. Fortunately, the roof is still damp and dripping, and I manage to rub my rag over it so as to suck out the remaining water. I sit back down and squash the damp cloth against my mouth, my nose; I rub my cheeks with it. It's amazingly good. This filthy liquid is better than anything I've had to drink before. Finally I slide a corner of the rag between my lips in order to suck it like a baby. From the sounds around me I guess that I'm not alone, that others must be doing the same thing. In the stinking darkness two, ten, fifteen thirsty babies are conscientiously sucking at the breast.

I close my eyes and am lulled by this unreal music.

I must have slept a little, for on opening my eyes again I see a bluish glow beyond the skylight. The last slat has gone from in front of the barbed wire. Someone has no doubt chopped it into small enough pieces to push it through the mesh to fall onto the tracks. As a result, the air is coming through and we can see the day dawning.

In front of the blue rectangle I can see two shadowy figures bringing a third up to it so he can breathe. The train continues on its way. So we must be going somewhere. You might even say it's pressing on, keen to arrive, and it's almost like wind coming into the wagon. But not enough to dispel the unbearable smell. Not enough either for us to get used to it. At the same time I tell myself that without the awful stink we would all have given up the ghost a long time ago. More than ever our dead comrades are protecting us. They're watching over us and making sure we keep alert.

I get up to help the two comrades to hold the weaker one. I take the place of one of them, who thanks me and goes to sit down. But there's nothing to thank me for; I'm doing my bit, thoroughly awake in this almost cold air. I can even watch the trees and fields going by;

I'd forgotten that such things existed, that a different scenery from the devastation of this wagon could exist, outside. That an outside could exist.

I don't know where we are, but it must be around six o'clock.

That makes twenty-four hours since we left the camp.

The air has brought the comrade round again, and we take him back. We're carried away by a glimmer of foolish hope.

All around shapes are beginning to move. Some stand up. Others, who had been propped up against others, straighten up carefully. I can see one creeping on all fours near the heap of bodies and disappearing behind it.

People are beginning to talk again. Each man checking his neighbour is alive.

Sounds of slapping ring out, and I'm worried that the recent madness is going to make a comeback; but it's a comrade trying to revive another who has passed out. He's begging him not to die, not to leave him. He tells him quietly that he can't do that to him. That he can't have held out until now only to go like that, to go now. When dawn has come and with the dawn, fresh air. After a few minutes he realises he's talking to a dead man, that he's been slapping a dead man. Then he sits down next to him, saying nothing, settles him across his knees and very gently caresses his hair.

All those still on their feet are circulating around the wagon, examining the grim group we make. A strange solidarity takes hold, at this time before the sun has risen and we can still forget the horrors of the previous day.

The crazy man who had been held up by his belt is dead. He's been put on top of the heap.

Using my rag, I clean the face of a young comrade, almost a child—I don't think I can be more than five years older than him but I feel so old now. I remember that he got into the train at Compiègne with his father, that a German had tried to separate them following some ridiculous order, but that they had resisted, they had held out despite being hit violently, first one, then the other, one protecting the other, in order to stay together, in order to confront together what they expected to be a distressing time, a difficult journey when they would need each other. A difficult journey.

I look around me for his father, but from the fixed stare of the boy I understand that the father has gone, that he's in the dark mass at the end of the wagon, in that shapeless swaying oozing mass. I'd like to encourage him, to find some words, but they don't come, so I concentrate on my bit of rag, focusing on wiping his forehead, his nose, his cheeks with a large black wound across them, blood still seeping from under the scab. I clean him up as I would a small child, I who have never known a small child, who will no doubt never have one. With the small amount of saliva I have left, I want to clean him up, I want him to look again like the child his father loved, that his father wanted to defend, to support to the end.

And he lets me do it.

He doesn't look at me.

I don't know what he's looking at.

Behind me a comrade is busy cleaning the floor with a handful of straw. He seems to put the same tenderness into it as I do into cleaning the young boy's face. The same distress, basically, for what's the good of cleaning this or that, this one or that one? You'd think we were waking up in a large dormitory, at the start of a day like any other day, wanting to start off clean and tidy.

Clean and tidy.

Someone suggests we do the count again. We do it, obediently. You wouldn't think that just a few hours ago there was a savage brawl going on here, a release of the horror which had been held back for too long.

And the strange refrain starts again, to the rhythm of the train:

"One."

"Two."

"Three."

"Four."

We're afraid it's going to stop too soon.

"Five."

"Ten."

"Fifteen."

"Twenty."

We wish it could go on to a hundred, as if the dead could count.

"Thirty."

"Forty."

"Fifty."

But the dead can't count. The dead will not be coming back. All the dead do is sway at the far end of the wagon.

"Fifty-one."

"Fifty-two."

"Fifty-three."

"Fifty-four."

"Fifty-five."

"Fifty-six."

We wait a moment. We hope. We're wrong to hope. So I tell myself, and tell myself again. We should have forgotten about hope a long time ago.

After fifty-six, there's nothing. Except silence. Fifty-six is the best we've been able to do, of what the night has left us.

Fifty-six of us are left.

Very happy to be one of those fifty-six.

The train continues on its way, but much more slowly than earlier. It's daylight now. We're taking it in turns again to be near the skylights. It's less hot than yesterday, but the atmosphere is still thick because of the corpses. At least we can nevertheless breathe more easily.

When it's my turn at the opening I concentrate on examining the countryside.

Well before the war I was in this area, at a children's summer camp near Bar-le-Duc. We must be getting near there. Just now there was a sign showing "Bar 38 km". I think I might perhaps recognise the place. There was a big lake, near the railway, where we came to swim. There were around thirty of us children, under the supervision of some adults who were strict but fond of us, who took good care of us. I have the impression it was in another life, a life which perhaps wasn't mine, and that perhaps I read about in a book and imagined so precisely that I came to believe it was my own life.

But I try to remember the book, and nothing comes to mind.

So I wait to see the lake.

Unfortunately, although I wish I could, I cannot monopolise the skylight just for myself. If the lake exists, no doubt I'm going to miss it.

After the thirst of the day before, now it's hunger beginning to torment us. Apart from the piece of bread distributed when we left, and the lump of sugar given to me by a comrade, I've had nothing to eat for over a day. I didn't touch the putrid sausage I'd also been given, and which got lost in yesterday's brawl.

After the brief calm of the early morning, anguish and rage are gradually mounting again.

I wish we'd arrive, or at least stop somewhere. I'd like to get out of this wagon. I notice I'm not the only one who's had enough, losing patience, longing to arrive at our destination wherever that might be.

Tension rises again when some start talking about escaping. I move towards the group who're putting this forward. I don't know any of them. Their idea is to make use of the holes which have been started in the floor, to increase them as far as possible, to pull up one or two planks, then to slide down under the train. Obviously in broad daylight it would be madness. Only three or four at the most could succeed before we were spotted on the track from the guard's van. And then we'd have had it, no doubt. But so what? Perhaps with a bit of luck? One of the group says loudly, "Why shouldn't we have a bit of luck this time?" I'm thinking, yes, why not? But then why would we have? And yet I don't care. I'd like to be one of those trying it. We're still in France; later, it will be too late.

But the less bold have also had a night's rest. And their complaints are the same as yesterday.

"You'll get us all shot!"

It becomes more heated, you can tell that the brawling could start up again. Nevertheless, our little group seems more determined than ever. We know we've nothing to lose. We say it. "We've nothing to lose now." But the others don't see it that way. They even dare to say they're not "terrorists".

I can't believe my ears.

They're defending themselves by saying they're not members of the resistance.

Where has that pretence of harmony gone, that apparent solidarity which had brought us together in the early morning? I feel crushed by a lead weight.

So there's nothing more?

Nothing to be saved?

On top of everything, one of those who want to stop us trying threatens to give us away. Someone raises a fist in his direction, but stops straight away, for fear of it all starting up again. Just the thought of the madness taking hold again, the presence of the heap in the corner of the wagon, are enough to stop it going any further.

The two sides pull apart, as far away as possible, knowing that's all they can do, conscious of the need to make sure it doesn't start up again. That that's the only thing that still matters.

After a moment we're all sitting again, our heads lowered; it's all too much.

I realise that the stimulation and then the anger had made me forget hunger and thirst. Now they're back, with even greater intensity.

Fortunately I'm distracted by the noticeable slowing down of the train. The brakes squeal, then the convoy comes to a complete stop. A comrade at the skylight says it must be a station. He can see a platform in front. Five or six others get up, crowd around the openings trying to see something. The silence is broken by the shouts of soldiers. Then nothing more.

That lasts for about fifteen minutes. We're all on tenterhooks. Someone who's managed to keep his watch says it's nearly midday.

Suddenly, without our hearing the guard's approach, the door opens, making us jump. We thought that was never going to happen. We thought it would never open, that we would remain there, locked away, until the end of time, until we became part of the heap.

The wagon fills with light and a blast of fresh air. From the grimace on the soldier's face we can see it's the opposite for him. He puts his head inside, sees the dark mass, hesitates for a moment, then bursts out cursing: "Schweine! Sie sind Schweine! Alle Schweine!", and then, with a strong Bavarian accent, to make sure we've understood, he explains: "All pigs!" Unbelievably his face makes me want to laugh. His surprised look, the silly fold of skin around his nose, the wrinkles in his forehead making his helmet slide down over his eyes, he's grotesque. Yes, we're all pigs wallowing in their filth, pigs amongst the slime and putrefaction. That's what we are. That's what you've turned us into. But you, standing there in disgust, you make me laugh. Your look of disbelief, with your nose turned up, is enough to make me die laughing, if I hadn't already died of hunger, of thirst, of horror. At least you've given me that, a laugh, inside myself, after all the horror.

Obviously that can't continue and we're glad very quickly to get your usual order, "Raus". It's so long since I heard that.

Yes, we're going to get out, and you can't imagine with what joy, what happiness, you who are already recoiling in front of us, you who are already turning your back to go and open another wagon to deliver other comrades whom you'll perhaps make laugh the way you've made me laugh, without knowing.

We climb with difficulty down to the track, the stronger ones helping the weaker.

And before the eyes of you German soldiers, we rediscover our dignity.

You, who wished to bring us down forever, to bring us down more and more, to relegate us to the level of beasts—and God knows, you've succeeded—now by your very presence, your stiff air of trained animals, you're giving us back a little of our humanity. In front of you we become men again, exhausted, brutalised, haggard, but men even so. Far from your eyes, in that dark filthy belly you threw us into, we could crawl and wallow, but in front of you we stand erect, or almost; we're no longer grovelling, or not quite.

I see the young comrade whom you've robbed of his father carrying one of those who perhaps got me out of the brawl yesterday.

I see the tall fellow who frightened me holding out his hand to one who's limping.

I see one whose hand is no more than a bloody rag supporting one who's staggering.

I see one who ten minutes ago was suffocating with an asthma attack trying to breathe calmly in order to guide one who can no longer see.

The blind man and the cripple.

You made us into a parable. We're turning that against you.

A parable that I could take with me to hell, because it would help me to get out of hell on my feet. Limping too, but on my feet.

It was not the Angel of Death I was fighting last night.

Or not the right one.

❁

As we climb down from the wagon the Germans are counting us, to be sure there won't be any missing when we set off again. They're too attached to us. As the track is too narrow, they make us go around the other side of a small ditch, in a field of potatoes where they've set up machine guns to ensure no one escapes. We sit down on the soft ground and watch the other wagons being emptied. On all sides comrades are climbing down, dazed, scared, unbelievably frail; but the number of survivors varies. Here, I count around twenty; there, more than seventy. And in the wagon where I would have been, if I had not changed my group at Compiègne, in the wagon which should have been mine, it's worse than I could have imagined. A single man gets out. One man. No one can believe it, but that's what we're seeing: the door is wide open, and a single man gets out.

A single man.

A single man out of the hundred who left.

One out of a hundred.

And still . . . His eyes are so large there's no expression to be seen in them. When one of our group tries to speak to him, he opens his mouth several times without managing to say anything. Nothing comes out. Nothing will come from the mouth of someone who has seen what he's seen, experienced what he's experienced.

I repeat to myself that I should have been in that wagon; I tell myself that, again and again; I should have been there, in that steel wagon where the heat must have been more atrocious than in any of the others; I tell myself that what we've experienced is nothing, since there are still fifty-six of us, fifty-six in a bad way but still fifty-six.

And suddenly I think about the man who took my place in that wagon. The first to change group with me, on the way to the station. Who is there now, in a heap which must be much bigger than the one in our wagon, bigger and less well arranged. At least in our wagon there were enough of us to stack them up properly.

But he was all alone . . .

Alone.

❋

Since we realised what has happened we can't take our eyes off that wagon, nor off that other one that the Germans have refused to open. We try to imagine what must be inside there.

Rain starts to fall again, distracts us a little. Quite soon we're squelching in mud, but only too happy to be squelching. We turn our faces up to the sky, opening our mouths wide to take in a few drops. Some are quick to dip their heads into the ditch between the field and the railway track. The Germans let them get on with it.

We were nearly all naked but several of us have managed to find trousers, either our own or those belonging to some of the dead, bigger or smaller men judging by the size of the trousers; we look like a crowd of zombies in too short, too long or ill-fitting pants. By chance, I've found my own. They're already soaked in rain, and black slime is running onto my feet, more slimy than the slime we're walking in which it mixes with. We make a strange, haunting spectacle.

That must be what a farm worker thinks as he cycles along a path through the fields and stops, dumbfounded, about a hundred metres away. He looks at us as if he's seen ghosts, an army of ghosts. I tell myself he's not totally mistaken. But he's roused by the shout of a soldier ordering him to turn back, aiming his rifle at him. The other, scared, takes flight, even forgetting to get back on his bike which he carries as he runs away.

The spectacle is reversed.

We're watching the man who'd been watching us.

You'd think he was in a scene from a Buster Keaton film, without the music.

The respite doesn't last long. The soldiers designate several of us to get the bodies out of the wagons where there are not so many and to pile them up into the others. I'm one of those designated. I'm lucky not to be sent to my own wagon, or worse, to the steel wagon, but to a wagon where the comrades did a bit better. In it there are only seventeen bodies, but I know now that in others there must be seventy or eighty or even more.

To start with we remove the corpses carefully. Partly decomposed, disfigured by the heat or by blows they're starting to come apart. The Germans in disgust force us to speed up, so that soon we're having to throw them onto the tracks. Limbs are breaking, heads splitting open, bellies emptying out onto the embankment. In the darkness it was horrible; but in the daylight . . .

I try not to look, but to act like a machine. I'm carrying sacks, not the bodies of my comrades.

But reality comes back to me in the form of a very distinct groan.

The one I'm carrying, who seemed so cold as I took his arms, isn't dead. He'd just got trapped under the heap. He might get out of this. So we handle him as gently as we can, taking every care as we put him tenderly down on the ground. It's a miracle we've been able to get him out alive. I find the handkerchief I'd left in my trouser pocket and start to wipe his face as I did for the lad in my wagon. But a violent blow from a rifle butt sends me reeling away from him. I don't have time to understand what's happening or to feel my shoulder when I hear a rifle shot.

They've finished him off.

Unable to do anything about it, rubbing my arm, I get back into the wagon to fetch the last body.

Meanwhile, other prisoners have been carrying out the reverse manoeuvre, loading those we've unloaded into the four front wagons. One lot are throwing bodies out, the others are throwing them in.

It's all well organised.

It's all very German.

On each of the four wagons a soldier chalks a number: 120, 120, 120 and on one, 121. It's almost perfect.

❅

I'm just finishing the mental calculation when an unlikely procession appears.

Three men, two of them carrying umbrellas, are coming towards us, almost running along the road, on ridiculous-looking legs. After the cyclist just now it's as if the circus is continuing. It's enough to make you forget what just happened, and the bits of bodies sticking to our hands.

We no longer know where we are.

One of the men, the one in the middle being protected by the umbrellas of the other two, thrusts his belly forward with its red stripe. It takes a moment to realise that it's a tricolour sash he's wearing. He confronts the first soldier who has stepped forward and addresses him nervously. The soldier, as surprised as we are by this rather peculiar group, indicates an officer close to me, perhaps the one who shot the dying man, or who gave the order to shoot.

I watch the three men approach, their faces red though you can't tell whether from anger, from having run through the rain, or from an excess of good health which seems out of place here. The one in the middle, the mayor of the local village no doubt, doesn't give the German a chance to open his mouth. He demands that the corpses from the convoy should be left with him; he wants to bury them in his cemetery, he repeats that he wants them here, in his cemetery, "on French soil"; he says they can't take them away just like that, contrary to the law. You'd think you were in a novel about chivalry.

But there's nothing chivalrous about our jailers.

After allowing the little man with the red face to finish his speech the officer replies calmly:

"All the deportees must arrive at the destination."

"But what about those who're dead?"

"All of them. Dead or alive. All. Without exception."

The mayor's expression is more incredulous than ever. Yet he insists bravely, he demands that the dead be given to him. "You can't do this."

I say to myself that they can do whatever they want, that they've done worse, that they've done everything, and I'm afraid for the little red-faced man.

The unbelievable thing is that since he arrived, beneath the ridiculous umbrellas of his deputy mayors, everything seems to have stopped. Everyone, soldiers and prisoners alike, or at least all those who have the strength to open their eyes, is staring at the strange trio. We're expecting one of the soldiers, or the officer, at any moment to take aim at these men who've appeared from another time, another reality than this one, and to dispatch them in the only way the Germans know how.

But the officer replies, amazingly without raising his voice.

Very calmly he proposes that the three men should get into the train to accompany "their" dead.

The mayor's face falls. He didn't expect such a response. He didn't expect such gentleness in such a response.

He hesitates. He lifts one foot. Then he turns without a word and walks away.

Like him, his deputies have gone pale, perhaps a little less brave, a little less ready to play the hero, remaining fixed to the spot. When they realise the mayor has gone they quickly turn and run after him.

End of diversion.

The comedy's over.

However, just when we thought we would be made to get back into the wagons, the officer gives the order for several of us to be sent to fetch water and provisions from the village. Once again a soldier picks me out, with a comrade. But this time I'm glad of it, despite my still sore ankle and my painful shoulder. I have an obscure feeling that getting away from this train might save me; I start to imagine who knows what, some improbable scenario.

They give us a sanitary tub to get filled up, from one of the wagons which were lucky enough to have one. First we empty it into the ditch. It doesn't bother us now. Then, accompanied by a soldier, we make our way towards the level crossing keeper's post. It's not very far to go, and if we have to come back that will be less tiring.

If we have to come back . . .

I realise I'm really beginning to think up a plan. I look at my comrade. But he doesn't lift his eyes in my direction. He can hardly stand. I don't know why they've picked him. His curly hair makes him look like a child, but his back is bent like an old man's. Quietly, I speak to him as we approach the house. He doesn't seem to hear me, unlike the soldier who with the flat of his hand—for once it's not a rifle butt—strikes me violently on the back shouting: "Ruhe!" What difference does it make to him if we talk? In any case, the other doesn't hear anything.

The level crossing keeper is a woman, I've only just noticed, who must have seen everything since the train stopped. She receives us without a word, but her face says more than anything we could say. She doesn't dare to smile at us, but we can see she wants to help us, to make a small sign, nothing much, just to encourage us in her way. But the soldier is there, and she doesn't know what to say, what to do. She points out the well to us.

I lean over it. I look at all that water. I look at what I've been dreaming of for hours. What could have saved us. What suddenly makes me feel faint.

The sound of the chain and the bucket bring me round.

For a brief moment I want to push the soldier into the well, to push him and run away. But I'm not even sure I have the strength to push him. And could my comrade help me? Would he even want to?

I watch the level crossing keeper turning the handle.

Has she understood? This time, she smiles at me.

That's all she can do. Smile at me. Not help me to push the German into the well. Once in the well, what then? What would happen? What could she do? What could all three of us do, by the well? Run? I don't even have any shoes anymore. And she has no reason to run away. I realise it all makes no sense.

A first bucketful has come up. The level crossing keeper would like to clean up the sanitary tub, but the soldier stops her, shouting, "Los! Los!" In any case, in the state that we are . . . we'll have to make do with this filthy water. And anyway, it can't make us any sicker than we already are.

Once our disgusting container is full, we have to get it back to the train. I realise that with my comrade as weak as he is it won't be easy. This water might save us later, but because it didn't do so earlier it's now breaking our backs.

We set off back to the train. There's nothing else to be done, no way out of it. No chance of escape. Nothing but the train. The wagon.

I haven't turned to thank the level crossing keeper. I haven't had the courage. But I can feel her watching us. Without seeing her, without having exchanged a single word with her, I know that she's as distressed as we are, that she would have liked to do something for us, that she would have liked to help us but that there was nothing she could do. At least she won't forget us. Not for a long time. Someone will remember us for a few days, perhaps for a few months.

And then?

My companion has stumbled. The tub almost tipped over. As I was taking most of the weight I've been able to avoid the worst. That doesn't stop the soldier striking the comrade, and this time with his rifle butt, shouting at him:

"Jude! Schmutziger Jude! Jude!"

His cries make me shiver. Instinctively I pull in my shoulders. I tell myself he's going to kill him, that perhaps he'll kill me next as I was the one who put the tub down on the ground. But an amazing thing happens. The other one gets up and yells in his turn at the soldier:

"Ich bin kein Jude! I'm a Christian! I'm a Christian!"

The soldier has stopped shouting. But the other continues. I tell myself he's mad, that this can't go on, that Jew or not, he'll get himself killed, he'll get us both killed. My hands are shaking, but he continues. He repeats that he's a Christian. Rather, that he was a Christian, that he was a Christian until yesterday, but now he's nothing. That now he's nothing. That the Germans have killed what he was, that they've killed Him in whom he believed and that they've killed him himself. That now he doesn't believe in anything. That he only believes in the Germans. That that's all that exists for him. The Germans and the devil. And he repeats it in the German's face, in his own language in his defiance:

"Ich glaube nur im Deutsche und Teufel. Deutsche und Teufel."

As incredible as it may seem the soldier says nothing. He hesitates. He keeps quiet. Looks at us. Then he looks at the tub at my feet. And points his rifle at me in quite a friendly way, saying simply:

"Wasser."

We take up our burden without a word. The comrade has calmed down. When we get to the train he helps me to hoist it up into a wagon that another German has indicated. My hands are still shaking. Fortunately the soldier sends us back into the field where the comrades who have witnessed the scene watch us wide-eyed. I sit back down in the mud. I fold myself in two. I grab my ankles with my hands to stop the shaking. I no longer know why I'm shaking. With cold, or fear. Until now I haven't been afraid. Or cold.

Time goes by like this. It's still raining, but not as hard.

I can't see anything.

I try not to think.

Not to expect anything. Not even the food we've been promised.

Nevertheless, a new group is coming along the road. Women, accompanied by soldiers. The Germans have refused to let men come with them. The only ones helping the women are the comrades who were sent to the village. A dozen of them are carrying large bowls. The women are following behind with baskets. We prefer not to imagine what might be inside them. When they all arrive at the train the soldiers dismiss the women.

The women hesitate at first.

Some are shifting from one foot to the other, like the mayor just now.

They look at us, helpless.

Then finally they leave.

We are ready to fall on the bowls and the baskets. Predictably, the soldiers make us line up.

Eventually they distribute a rather thin soup with a few vegetables hastily thrown in, scarcely cooked, and a raw potato for each man which the soldiers take from the baskets, helping themselves of course at the same time. In the end there aren't enough and we have to share them.

It doesn't matter.

It doesn't matter that the soup is too thin.

It doesn't matter that the potatoes are not cooked.

It doesn't even matter that there's not enough.

It's so much more than we've had so far. So much more than I'd dreamed of in this field.

Despite the persistent hunger several of us have got some colour back. Unbelievably I can even hear some laughter.

I remember the name of the village shown on the level crossing keeper's house: Révigny, like reverie, a name to dream of.

But the dream doesn't last. Soon we have to get back into the train. The Germans divide us amongst the eighteen wagons where there are no corpses.

The one I have to get into isn't the one I was in before and it's almost a relief. I've been put in with new comrades. The ones from my first wagon aren't here. It pains me not to be with them anymore, as if I've forgotten that some no doubt had wanted to kill me, as I'd wanted to kill them, to make more room, to have more air, more water. Death brings you closer together, especially the death you want to deal out.

But I don't have time to miss them. One of those giving me a helping hand to climb into my new wagon has recognised me and calls me by my real name, without thinking. Even though he's spoken quietly I curse him inwardly and pretend not to know him:

"Not Weismann. Vilar. I'm Vilar. I'm Swiss."

Fortunately, he doesn't insist. These days it's better if such meetings between friends don't take place.

I take advantage of the fact that we're less packed in to creep as far away as possible and by chance finish up by the front skylight. There are no more than seventy-three of us and we're almost comfortable. A dead man takes up less space than a living one and is easier to pile up; that's an advantage for those who are left. What worries me is that my new wagon is right behind the one that remained closed at Révigny. I can't help thinking of it, of all the comrades inside, all dead no doubt. No point in opening it, that's what the Germans must have said to themselves. At least they saved us that, having to decant a hundred corpses into the front wagons. I imagine that tomb on wheels in front of us, as if showing us the way. I suddenly tell myself that the smell will very soon become unbearable. I can't think of anything but that, the smell of all those bodies which the wind will soon be washing over us. I scold myself for not thinking of anything but that. But how can I think of anything else? How can I imagine only the faces of the living as they were just a few hours ago? They're now slowly melting into one single grimacing face, weeping from all its pores, a single subsiding mass, a single body from a hundred bodies, one flesh.

I'd prefer not to be thinking about this, but it won't go away. My memories are ineffective against the thought of what is moving along through the air in front of us. I try in vain to conjure them up, I try in vain to concentrate on something else. There's nothing to be done about that thing in front. That Thing is watching me, is inside myself. It won't let go of me, whatever I do.

We've scarcely been on the move for ten minutes when the train stops again. Nothing is said, but I'm sure we're all thinking the same thing, that we shouldn't keep stopping, we've got to finish this once and for all, that it doesn't matter what's awaiting us, we just want to get there, quickly, yes, to get it over with.

I don't know how to say this.

They've opened the wagon in front of us.

The others are crowding around me to watch. The skylights in my new wagon have kept most of their slats, which stops us seeing very much. We daren't pull them off whilst the train is at a standstill. Fortunately, two of them have a big enough gap between them for me to see some of what's happening in front.

I can't believe my eyes.

Miraculously comrades are climbing in an unending stream out of the wagon which I'd thought was full of dead bodies, amidst the yelling and the blows from rifle butts, boots and whips of the Germans. But none of them says anything. They're quite docile, following the soldiers, away from the track, tripping, picking themselves up, crossing the ditch, beneath the continuing blows and shouts, and exhausted, harassed and in rags they move away from the train.

Seeing the two machine guns being carried by their guards I suddenly realise what's happening. The miracle isn't going to last long. They're going to be shot. They must have tried to escape. The soldiers are taking them out of sight to do it. Not one will be left. What I was seeing in my head, what I was imagining in the darkness of the wagon, that's what they'll be in a few minutes' time by a path somewhere.

Everyone is quiet.

Everyone has understood.

And those leaving the train know what's ahead of them. We were warned.

One of them turns towards the train as if looking for us, then disappears with the others behind a bush along the path, followed by other comrades who don't even have the strength to look back at us, and are moving obediently on.

The last one has disappeared.

We wait in a heavy silence weighing down on us and I recall the same at Fresnes, the unbearable waiting for the sound of deadly rifle fire.

How much time goes by? Impossible to know. It's unending. There we are, straining to hear, waiting for the rattle of machine gun fire. A comrade behind me has started praying aloud and one or two others join in with him. I can't help thinking that no prayer can save, or even help, those who've gone that way. A few hours ago I think I might have envied them. But now a great wave of pity comes over me, a great wave of sadness, for them, for me, for us all. Having suffered all that, just to end up at the side of a field.

If the journey lasts another two days there won't be anyone left alive in the train. They'll have killed us all, or let us kill each other, before piling us up in these wagons like a huge mobile cemetery.

None of it makes any sense.

Why didn't they execute us at Fresnes or at Royallieu?

Perhaps they couldn't bury us there?

Perhaps the cemetery is the train's destination?

Perhaps that's where they're taking us, that that's what the train's for, a long funeral procession of twenty-two wagons, so we can be buried far away, without anyone seeing us, without anyone knowing where?

If not, what's this all about?

Inside the wagon the silence continues, hanging over us, intolerable.

We start to hope for the sound of firing, to put an end to it. To put an end to the waiting. To put an end to everything. Yes, for an end to everything once and for all. For them. For us.

Then a second miracle happens: a comrade reappears, then two, then three, then the whole wagon we'd thought were finished; they're leaving the path, crossing the ditch, doing the journey in reverse, as if nothing had happened. The soldiers are still barking, still randomly hitting out at shoulders, heads, backs, but our comrades are there, alive, moving towards their wagon. We don't understand what's going on, we can't believe our eyes, our ears. It's as if they've come back from the dead, twice, to leave the wagon and then to get back into it, with the same docility each time. Then suddenly a shot brings us back to reality, as happens each time we think there might be hope, joy, belief again in something, in mankind.

Two Germans appear carrying a body.

Just one.

They've only killed one. It doesn't seem like them, but they've only killed one. Is that the miracle?

The wagon in front is full again, with a very small amount of extra space. The door closes again.

Immediately the train sets off again, slowly. It drags itself along, like its cargo. You'd say it too is stumbling, jolting to a stop, restarting, stopping again, hiccupping, with us inside, prisoners once more of the suffocating heat. But this time we stand up to it and keep our clothes on, those we've been able to get back, so that the sweating doesn't kill us, doesn't drive us mad. Having a little bit more space helps us to breathe a bit better.

It doesn't stop one of our number dying soon, without saying anything. And we don't say anything either. Death has become commonplace, and this one was so gentle, hardly noticeable . . .

Two comrades lay the body down in a corner, as we've done so many times before.

Now we're seventy-two plus one dead body. The train continues on its way.

❋

We arrive at Bar-le-Duc. I haven't seen the lake from my childhood.

The station is almost empty. In the blocks of flats overlooking the tracks we can see curtains being lifted, timidly. Between the wooden panels of my skylight I can see two windows, one above the other, and in each window frame silhouettes can be made out. You'd say our train is not passing unnoticed. And yet they must have seen such trains passing for a quite a time. But ours is not a train like the others. The smell coming off it must attract the attention of all those who have become used to the sight of the trains, all those no longer surprised to see prisoners' fingers at the barbed wire of the skylights, the outstretched hands, the black faces in the wagons.

They've seen it all. For all time, to the end of time. Privileged spectators of everyday horror.

Except that with us, the horror is not everyday horror.

Our horror is like nothing else.

That's what they must be saying to themselves.

No need for shots at these windows, no need for the silhouettes of overly curious people to be made to disappear for them to understand. Our spectacle is not like the others.

No witnesses for us.

We're passing by incognito, so to speak. No one must know about us.

Would the Germans finally be ashamed? I don't believe so. There must be other reasons. Nothing can ever redeem them. Even shame.

If, after the train has been rolling along quite slowly for a few minutes, it stops again, this time in a siding, far from prying eyes, it's for an obscure military or political reason. Not to escape men's judgement for what they're doing to us. That at least I'm sure of, even if I don't understand what they're doing to us or why.

❋

After less than a quarter of an hour we set off again.

For the thousandth time, perhaps, we're off again.

Stopping. Starting. Stopping. Starting. For two days that's all we've done.

We're getting used to it. Obviously, you can get used to anything.

Soon it will be dark.

We're going to spend our second night in this train. At least we'll have spent a second day with only one death in the wagon. It's almost unbelievable.

In my new wagon men hardly talk. No doubt the first part of the journey has removed for a long time any inclination for discussion. And yet I feel more than ever that that's all that's left to us, words. And maybe tomorrow it will too late. Or even in an hour.

Yet the train continues on in the gathering darkness, and none of us has died since Bar-le-Duc.

It can't be far off ten o'clock in the evening when someone notices a board for "Novéant". Another, who must be my age, if that, says in a bright, naïve way that I didn't think it possible to hear again, replies straight away:

"Hey, chaps! It's where I live . . ."

Another one passing his home, no doubt never to return. As if our train is determined to give back to all these men a little of their past life so they'll better understand that it's well and truly over.

"It's where I live I tell you. How funny."

Funny. Another word I thought I'd never hear again. For him, it's funny being here.

And an irony of fate. Our wagon stops right opposite the house where he was born. And now we can't stop him. He talks, and talks, doesn't stop talking, as if that can reconnect him to what he's going to leave forever. He tells us how his parents came to settle there, after the other war, how his father chose this house beside the station so he could watch the trains, because even as a little boy he'd been mad about trains, they were his dream that he wanted to be able to see every day. The way a man who's keen to travel but will never leave goes to live at a port so he can watch the transatlantic liners and imagine leaving with them. Everyone to his own dreams. His own impossibility. This one must have seen plenty of trains passing. I can't help being glad for him that he died at the time of the Popular Front—died of joy, his son told us, slightly nostalgically. One of our group expresses doubt that you can die of joy, but the other insists. Heart attack, he says. He was too happy. To die of happiness, it makes you wonder, in our situation. In any case, he's dead and at least death has spared him our train and all those trains that have been passing for months.

However, his mother is still alive . . . The heart-rending thought that his mother is perhaps there, watching us, suddenly plunges him into silence which none of us wishes to break.

Astonishingly, floodlights have been directed at the convoy. No doubt they're expecting another escape attempt. Suddenly discretion is off the agenda. We are all that's illuminated in the darkness, along with the shapes still moving around on the platforms who sometimes cross through the halo of light before disappearing back into the dark.

The comrade suddenly breaks his silence. He's recognised two of the railway workers. As a boy, his father used to take him along when he went for a drink with them and both of them, father and son, with the son already playing at being a "grown up", listened to talk of travels as if they'd been those of the heroes of antiquity. From what he says, Ulysses or Aeneas had no greater prestige in his eyes; and at least you could go for a drink with the railwaymen.

Yet, if his heroes haven't changed, he notices that their caps have: now they're the German railway caps, a detail that sets him off thinking again, whilst the train starts again slowly towards another siding.

We hardly have any time to wait for something to happen. The floodlights are off, but we can hear the footsteps of many soldiers and shouted orders that echo in the deserted station.

After a while the door is flung open. This time the smell of rotting flesh comes from outside, from the front wagons where the corpses have been piled up. To say that our wagon smells good . . .

An officer is there, whip in one hand, a torch in the other. He asks if there are any dead. We say yes. One. "Get him out." We carry him to the door and two soldiers grab hold of him, no doubt to take him to the front wagons. Then the officer forces us to crowd into one end of the wagon, leaving a small empty space, and starts to count us: a lash of the whip on each back, and we move to the other end.

One lash, one man.

One lash.

One man.

One lash.

One man.

Some can't help but cry out. Even if you expect it, even if you prepare yourself for it, you can't get used to that pain.

One lash. Then another. And another. And as many men are counted and move to the other end. Almost as many men cry out.

After a while, as the count gets to forty and the two groups are about the same size, he's between the two halves, in the semi-darkness of the wagon. We're surrounding him, a dark mass, darker than the night.

Suddenly I imagine us all throwing ourselves on top of him, crushing him, stamping on him, massacring him, tearing him to pieces in the darkness and confusion. Then our nails wouldn't be lacerating our own bodies, our fingers wouldn't be covered in our own flesh, our mouths full of our own blood. He'd be the one, not us, being destroyed by kicks, fists, teeth, the one who'd be submerged under the horror and wretchedness into which they've plunged us. With what joy I would turn his hatred against him, with what joy I would tear out his eyes, I would crush his vile face which can't help spitting out a "dirty Jew" to one comrade or another who disgusts him more than another as he sends him to the other end.

And too bad if afterwards they come and shoot the lot of us.

✹

But that's an image that remains in my head, we don't do anything.

As my turn comes I take the lash on my back and pass into the other half of the wagon, docile and silent.

We're still at seventy-two.

The door closes again.

We're almost relieved not to be getting the smell of decomposition in our faces. Now it's the turn of the next wagon.

In the darkness we comfort some of the older ones who're suffering more than others from this last gratuitous blow to their exhausted bodies. Then we try to settle down for the night, packing ourselves in as best we can, fitting round each other, heads to feet in this big communal bed of shared suffering. It's a long time since we were bothered about the bugs on the floor, though we can't get used to the smell still pervading the wagon and all around the train.

From where I'm lying I'm lucky enough to see a slight glow through the skylight. I try to believe it's a rising star that will soon be lighting up the sky.

I'm surprised to be glad that we didn't do anything just now, when we could, even with no hope; I'm glad that the image stayed in my head, that we didn't trample the beast as he deserved. Whatever we are, whatever we do, we'll always be stronger than them, for we're more human. Strangely, I tell myself that it's our suffering which stops us being like them, stops us being them, ever being them. They'll never experience the suffering they've inflicted on us. If they were to experience it I believe—now that the alarm has passed—that I would fight to prevent it. It would bring us down to their level, and we would lose all that's left to us.

We are not them.

We are not them.

The master race. We'll never be part of it.

I know I belong to the race of those who are beaten, who are massacred for all time, those who are whipped and thrashed, those who cry out from the depths of the abyss, those who are tortured to death, those who are denied, those who are ground down but who rise again, those who are bowed down but not broken, those who remain standing amidst the flames, those they cannot banish from their nightmares, those who will be there until the end of time to remind them that we are not them. I don't know what will become of us a day from now, a month, a year. A century from now. What trace will remain of what is happening to us. Who will be there to tell the story. But even as they try to eradicate us, we shall be there in the midst of them. I'll be one of those who'll never leave them, reminding them forever that we are not them. That we are not of the same race, the same species. That we shall always resist being what they are. Even when dead. Especially when dead. I want to be the resistance to them, even when dead, and never be like them. That's what I want to be. That's what I am. And I go to sleep, gently lulled by a wave of images coming back to me as if from an old book.

❊

The waves are suddenly rising and from the sea comes the cry of a child. I lean over the side of the boat; I see the child, wrinkled, hideous, disfigured and I hear his wails coming up from the abyss. His cry, the sea, a single roaring sound, and I want to drag him from the depths, despite the horror I feel. I don't know who he is. I don't know why he's crying out. All I know is that I want to pull him out of the water, to stop him crying, so that I can hear the sea again as before, without cries, without tears. I'd like to hear the sea coming up the beach as it did when I was a child. I'd like to see the sea without the child there. But the child is struggling in the depths, in the sea. And in the sea is a burning city and I can see his body squirming. I can see his mouth grimacing. He's a hundred years old. He's a thousand years old. I don't know how old he is, but I know he's crying and squirming in the city burning at the bottom of the sea and I wish he'd disappear. I wish there were no city, no child, no flames. I hit out at the sea. I hit out at the city in flames. I hit out at the child's face. The water becomes cloudy, but the face keeps coming back, and the city, and the flames, and the sea. I hit out, but the face comes back, the face grimaces, the flames at the bottom of the sea. But the sea draws back, taking the cries. The cries recede with the sea, and the flames with the sea. There's just the beach and the sand. The child has gone, and the flames with the sea. The beach has come back. And the sand on the beach. But the beach is covered in grass. The grass covers the wet sand in tufts, in clods, in huge dirty patches. The beach has gone. I have to walk on the grass in the middle of the wet sand. I scream at the beach covered in grass, this rotten beach, this beach being destroyed by the grass. I want to walk once again on damp sand, feeling the little waves hardening under my feet. But there's nothing left but a field of grass and sand, a field of sodden sand covered in grass. I lie down in the grass and the sand and weep for the lost beach. I sleep a dreadful sleep. But I sleep knowing that I sleep. I sleep to forget the lost beach, the lost sea, the lost child who cried in the sea, in the flames, in the city beneath the sea.

I wake up; it has been light for a while. It must be seven or eight o'clock. In fact, I don't care what time it is. I'm enjoying the motion of the train which has got going again. I listen to the sound of the wheels, a strangely friendly sound. I'd like to go back to sleep, a dreamless sleep, a sleep to get me away from my dreams. And I listen to the sound of the wheels.

Shush, shush, the sound of wheels in my head.

Shush, shush, the sound of wheels on the rails.

Shush, go to sleep, it sings to me. Go to sleep, says the dreamless song. Shush, sleep, your father's going to the village. Shush, sleep, he'll bring you an apple. And your head will feel better. And your head will be better.

Shush, sleep, he'll bring you a walnut.

And your foot will be better.

And your foot will be better.

Shush, sleep, he'll bring you a bird.

And your eyes will be better.

And your eyes will be better.

The song goes around in my head, not in the dream; it goes round and round and my heart is full. I must wake up. I must wake up. But the wheels are turning and the words are flowing, worse than tears. *Wejn nischt, wejn nischt, klejner josem.* Don't cry, don't cry, little orphan. Hold on to your tears in your misery. Hold on to your tears like diamonds. You'll need them one day. *Wejn nischt, wejn nischt, klejner josem.* My eyelids are heavy, my eyes are full. My eyes are hurting. I need to open them.

A comrade is watching me. To start with I think it's the child from the dream again. But he holds out a piece of cloth, a rag, remnant of a shirt or handkerchief. I realise my face is wet. I guess I've been crying, and I'm ashamed. I who have seen so many horrors in such a short time, I'm ashamed that I've been crying in my sleep. But the comrade smiles and I pack away my pride and try to smile back. After all, that's something else that differentiates us from our guards. We cry, we cry like children, we cry the way the child in my dream cried, we even cry in our sleep, we can still cry, still dream, still have nightmares, dream dreams that we don't understand, remember lullabies we thought we'd forgotten, cry at our dreams. That too makes us not like them. Or do they cry too? Do they still cry? Do they still think of their mothers? Their fathers? I don't believe so. Yesterday morning one of us, a young man, called to a soldier through the skylight, begging him to help an older man who was dying, asking him to remember his own father, to help in the name of his father, to give him water, to save this old man who was dying and could have been his father. But the other replied in bad French: "Me no father. You kill him."

For him, that was enough.

He no longer had a father. No need to remember. No need to remember anything. No need to think of anything. He no longer had a father. Perhaps no mother. And that was enough for him.

And what should I say?

But I don't want to think about my parents.

Fortunately, it's my turn at the skylight. I use it to concentrate on some of the names on the boards as they go by. They're already all in German, and yet we're still in France. At least, in what used to be France. We must have passed Metz. I take advantage of the air coming in to "refresh" myself a little, despite the heat which is mounting again. I can't help thinking that I didn't choose a very good season to get caught, I've never liked the heat except at the seaside. But the sea is far from here; it's only in my dreams, and in my dreams it burns.

Once again, despite our reduced numbers, despite the holes that have been made in the wagon, we're threatened with suffocation. In addition, this time we know what will happen if it all starts again. In order to prevent the air becoming foul too quickly and sparking off madness in us, we keep our clothes on, or rather the rags we were able to gather at Révigny. They'll catch the sweat. Never has the expression "Once bitten, twice shy" made more sense—or rather, "A scalded cat fears hot water" as we've been more scalded than any cat, and it's our blood that's boiling in our weakened brains.

One of us, however, has started telling stories in order to drive out the fear which is taking hold of us, or simply to calm us down. How can he do that? How can he still tell stories? His repertoire seems inexhaustible. I admire the man's strength at least, his force of character which from the depths of the abyss is captivating the herd we've become. I wonder how long he can go on, as I listen as quietly as all my comrades. We are all so old now, whatever age we were before we got into this train, and here we are listening to him like children being comforted in the dark. Will it be enough to keep us alive?

We shall find out later; we're arriving at a station and the storyteller goes silent.

Someone says, "Sarrebourg!"

I hear "Strasbourg". And my heart tightens to think of the frontier being so close.

The train doesn't move, and I only understand my mistake half an hour later. The screams of two Germans have us jostling to try to see what's going on; beneath the Sarrebourg signboard two officers are violently arguing. We can't believe our eyes or our ears, but it cheers us up no end. If the Germans are screaming at each other . . .

Perhaps they'll finish up by fighting? We begin to hope so.

We'd like to know what they're saying, and those amongst us who speak their language the best try to translate for us. But they've lowered their voices, suddenly conscious of our presence. The fun will be for another time . . . And very quickly the good humour vanishes and we go back to thinking about the mounting heat. But we're saved from sinking back into despair by the Red Cross caps which some have caught sight of.

And we have good reason not to sink back into despair.

For, whilst some in their state of despair are claiming that it will be like the first day, at Soissons, that the torture will start again like on the first day, that they're going to make us believe in hypothetical kind souls coming to look after us, the door opens.

It's extraordinary.

In front of us are three women in nurses' uniforms.

So are they going to take care of us, really? So is someone still thinking of us, a little? So do we still exist? So have we not been totally forgotten?

The door has opened, and hope came in first. But what we quickly see in the eyes of these women frightens us. For what we see is what we've become.

We see ourselves in their unbelieving looks.

We see what our guards have turned us into; we see it more clearly than if we were looking at ourselves in a mirror.

At Révigny we didn't see anything. We were too exhausted, too afraid, coming back from too far away, to properly look at ourselves, or to really look at those who were looking at us without understanding. And the rain hadn't helped. But in these six eyes fixed upon us it's the truth of what we've become that sees us and we are able to look it in the face.

It only lasts for a moment. Just enough time to think it would have been better not to see anything.

It only lasts for a moment, but it hits us hard.

And we'd prefer to close our eyes. We would, they would.

They'd like to close their eyes so as not to see the horror that has been done to the men we are. That we were.

We'd like to close our eyes so as not to see the horror of what we've become.

❋

But we have to keep our eyes open.

So we keep our eyes open. They do, and we do.

And what helps us to keep our eyes open is what's in the bowls on the platform behind the nurses. Soup. That is to say, water with something to eat in it. A little something. What we've been missing for the past twenty-four hours.

So obviously we don't spend much time looking into the eyes of the nurses. We don't spend much time looking into their scared eyes. Very quickly we're looking at the bowls behind them, and at what's in them. Too bad what they've seen. Too bad what we've seen. We're going to have something to drink and eat. That's all that matters.

And the distribution begins.

It takes time to feed so many wretched men. But time, that's all we have. So we wait, almost patiently. But when our turn comes we're carried away by joy, a noisy, violent, fierce joy. A cruel joy.

You'd think we were at a New Year's Eve fete, full of children jostling around the stands, stretching out their hands to carefree mothers—but a terrible, monstrous fete, with scrawny children stretching out their hands not for sweets, not for sugary treats which they'll never again taste, but for these strange cardboard small cylindrical cartons they receive in return and which they grab eagerly. Cartons full of a strange mixture which they enjoy without a second thought.

Naturally we'd prefer something refreshing, something which doesn't add more heat to the heat already killing us, already causing grimacing railwaymen to be shovelling lime onto what's oozing out of the front wagons. But we eat it anyway, we drink, we suck the cartons. We swallow it all.

The soup is spicy. It's too hot. It makes us thirsty. But it's soup. We ask for more.

We shout.

We shout for more.

We shout. We call for more.

But in vain.

We knew it of course. The Germans aren't going to allow us this kindness.

They shove the nurses aside, slam the doors shut, in a hurry to get moving. To get moving and be finished with it.

Then, as the train slowly sets off again, we see the women holding out wet cloths, holding them out to us at the barbed wire mesh, holding them out to our eager hands trying to grab them, our hands which the speed soon puts out of reach.

And they're running, as if we're a vision, holding out their cloths, running in desperation as if we're He in whom they believe perhaps, like nuns with their wimples. As if we're He who wept upon the cross, begging in David's voice, uttering His last piercing cry: why have you abandoned me?

Why have you abandoned me?

This cry like a chant that's taken up by the wheels with their monotonous rhythm. This chant of the wheels like a song of David.

Esther enters the first court.

Esther enters the second court.

Esther enters the third court.

Esther enters the fourth.

Close is the anguish, there is no help. Many bulls surround me.

Their jaws gape around me like roaring, mauling lions.

I'm sliding away like water and my bones are dislocating.

My strength is as dry as a shard of glass.

My strength, and my mouth. Like a shard of glass. Burnt by the soup. Burnt by thirst. Burnt by agony. And my dry tongue. Like a shard of glass. My tongue is hard in my mouth. Harder than my heart will ever be.

The wheels turn on the rails. I stop myself crushing the empty cardboard cornet. I sense already that I shall need it. Everything is useful for someone who has nothing left but words in his head, a few memories, a few sentences that come back to him.

I close my eyes and let the sentences resonate. My head is an echoing cavern. I try to stay still, not thinking of anything, especially not of that too spicy soup which is making me so thirsty, that soup which is torturing me and taking over my belly, my whole body. I'm at the bottom of my cavern. It's hot. I'm suffocating. And suddenly air comes in. But it doesn't last. As I'm away from the skylight I keep my eyes closed. There's nothing to see. We've passed Sarrebourg. Germany is not far away now.

So I stay in my cavern. I try to remember my sentences. My strength like a glass shard. My dry mouth. No help. And again, a draught of air coming in. Fresh air in my head. No help.

I open my eyes, it's totally dark. I don't understand anything. I didn't think I'd gone to sleep. But the hours go by, and everything gets confused . . . And then daylight suddenly comes back, as if there'd been an eclipse. I'm so dazed that it takes me a while to realise that we're simply going through a series of tunnels. Here's another one; I get the impression that the train accelerates when it comes to it. Is the driver perhaps thinking about us? After all, why not? Unless the man in charge has just told him speed up, to get away from the smell we're dragging along after us.

But we don't worry about it anyway, whether it's a stink or a pleasant fragrance.

I laugh at myself for having such ideas, such thoughts in my head. A head stuffed full of hopeless junk, this burden I've inherited from my school masters. Or else a distraction to reduce the suffering? I would love to have a clear out. Empty the cavern for good. So there'll be nothing left but emptiness and fresh air.

The fresh air, however, has been left behind us, in the tunnels. Beneath the blazing sun we get back to our normal demeanour—the demeanour of a funeral procession, this time the cliché comes into my head of its own accord; and the cavern is no nearer to being empty than the wagons of this train.

Even if it makes me seem like a show-off I decide to run through in my head all the *départements* and their county towns to keep my memory in working order. It keeps me occupied for a little while and I'm pleased I do so well, telling myself at the same time that it really hasn't done much good to have remembered all that. If I'm going to die soon I won't have got to know even one tenth of these regions; and even most of those I have seen will have been when I was armed or undercover, that is to say, without really having seen anything of them. For me, they were reduced to strategic "points" on maps: Gestapo posts, offices of the pro-Nazi *Milice*, German arms depots, resistance hiding places, friendly farms, hostile farms, dubious villages, suspect town halls, more or less trustworthy priests, bakeries where messages could be left, groceries to be avoided, or vice versa. I have my own little map with my own modest high points or my monuments to horror. The next stops will probably all be in the latter category.

Almost out of geographical curiosity at the next station I ask a bit too loudly if anyone knows where we are. After looking round for a moment, the comrade by the skylight replies: Haguenau. And another chips in straight away: around forty kilometres from Strasbourg.

Forty kilometres. The countdown is underway. We'll soon be seeing the end of that ball of string we wanted to be unwound as quickly as possible.

124

I'm not sure we still want it unwound.

We'd prefer to stay here until nightfall.

I don't know anything about Haguenau, but I do know it's on the right side of the Rhine. That's all I want to know about it and it pleases me. For once, the train leaves again almost straight away. Obviously they're keen to arrive. To get rid once and for all of us and our smell. The smell of their crime.

Then, since I can't empty out what is in the cavern of my head, and to keep things in working order, I try to work out the speed of the train and the amount of time it will take to reach Strasbourg. As I'm at a distance from the opening I watch the shadows passing on the right-hand side; I do my best to distinguish between trees and electricity poles, contrasting in my imagination the bushiness with the slenderness, sorting the wheat from the chaff. My eyes are fixed wide open, almost haggard, and when I ask my neighbour what the distance might be between two electric poles, I notice he's looking at me anxiously. It dawns on me suddenly that he thinks I've gone mad, that he thinks the madness of the first day is going to take hold of me again, and perhaps others with me. That perhaps it's going to start up again.

I reassure him and explain my calculations.

A smile briefly crosses his face.

He tells me he's a teacher in a little village in the Nièvre area. Stupidly, we shake hands as if meeting socially, which brings the fleeting smile back to his lips. He must have had the same idea as me. Two madmen in a train; one of them counting shadows. How do you do?

Suddenly he starts counting with me. He tells me he recalls setting an exercise involving the distance between electricity poles, and that the distance stated was eighty metres between each pole. He doesn't know if that's correct but it seems likely to him. I tell him that it seems likely to me too. We decide on eighty metres. We have nothing to lose. As neither of us has a watch, and as in the end it's just part of the game we've just invented, we share the work: he'll count the seconds, and I'll count the presumed poles. We give ourselves five minutes to get an average count.

The game begins. One. Two. Three.

We apply ourselves like two schoolboys at the blackboard. I can't help saying this to him, and the idea tickles him so much that he loses concentration and we have to start again.

Once more the imaginary seconds go past in his head, whilst I scrutinise the shadows passing as if at a run and which I like to believe are electricity poles: ten, fifteen, twenty poles; I concentrate hard, but I can't help thinking about that other count taking place a few hours ago as the living took the places of the dead. But I keep going; I dismiss the image, or rather I settle it in its place, beside me, silent, keeping with me as I count, quietly letting me get on with it, slightly ominous, but I keep going, thirty-two, thirty-three, I'm counting poles, I'm counting time going by, thirty-nine, I count life, the life that's left to us, forty-one, the space that's left to us before we pass to the other side, forty-two, forty-three, and when he says "stop", when he stops his interior clock after our five minutes, I've just said "forty-four".

That is, a passenger train in five minutes passes in the region of forty-four electricity poles approximately eighty metres apart, so what would be the likely speed of the train? You don't need to take into account the number of dead in each wagon.

I shouldn't have let myself become distracted, for suddenly I've lost track. But this time my comrade's smile lights up his whole face: "We're doing 42.3 kilometres an hour!" I smile in my turn. If I haven't been able to empty my head, I've at least helped my neighbour to recapture some of his previous life. I congratulate him warmly on the speed and precision of his calculations, admitting miserably that he's left me behind (if only that were true).

Buoyed up by having found the answer, we wonder how long it was after leaving Haguenau that we started counting. And we come to the conclusion that, if we don't stop in the meantime, we should be at Strasbourg in less than half an hour.

We're not exactly delighted by the news. I would prefer it if he were wrong.

But a schoolteacher, like a hussar even when he's fallen off his horse, doesn't get things wrong. In under half an hour we shall be on the other side of the Rhine.

On the other side.

The worst of it is that our comrades have kept up with our little calculation. Everyone knew perfectly well that it wouldn't be long, but to put a figure like this on the time left to us before the frontier makes it all more obvious, almost tangible. Yes, soon we'll be able to touch it, we'll be there, we'll finally be able to set foot there whether or not we're still standing. This idea has been with us since the start, but now suddenly it's taken on the weight of unbearable reality, and something breaks inside us for good.

And a pushing and shoving starts, nothing serious but nevertheless full of confused anguish: we all, such as we are, have the feeling that it will soon be too late; we want to see our country for the last time, even the few foreigners amongst us and for whom France will perhaps be their last homeland. Each man fixes his eyes on what he can see before giving up his place to the next man—a glimpse of roof, a tree, a small stretch of road, a field, a ditch, and for the luckier ones a church with its clock tower, a little less sad than the rest. For myself I see something I'd rather not have seen: two women at the entrance to a bridge, waving as they watch us, two women saying goodbye to this indistinct mass of the train in which they can imagine the men we are, sense the corpses accompanying us and those we shall perhaps be this evening, perhaps tomorrow. The handkerchiefs they hold to their noses are not for tears. But they wave, and that's enough for me.

Giving up my place to a comrade who pushes me away rather roughly, I slide along the wall; I close my eyes, taking with me their hands still waving behind my eyelids.

✦

At Strasbourg the train doesn't stop, and that's so much the better. It plunges quickly onto the Kehl bridge, at least according to what one of our group says who seems to know the place.

We can hear the wheels echoing in the empty space.

A faint voice starts to sing the Marseillaise, and soon twenty, thirty, seventy-two voices take it up, wavering at first, then not wavering, refusing to waver, as our legs are all at once holding firm, determined to stay strong above this empty space, between France and that country that the Allies will soon destroy, we're sure of that.

For they'll destroy it.

We know they'll destroy it. Just after, or just before, we've been destroyed, they'll destroy it. I only just rejoice at the thought when the sound of our song swells, intensifies beyond measure, roars louder than the wheels of the train and the rolling of the river. So loud, you'd think the whole train is singing with us. And all the train is singing with us.

We're singing like madmen.

Like desperate men.

We're singing for nothing.

The way cattle low.

Yes, we're foolishly singing that song I've always hated then learned to love at the worst moments, and this moment is the worst. We're singing at the tops of our voices, this song has become our only haven, the only refuge where we're all as one. We're singing "like one man", we're really a single voice, a single suffering body. We're just one man, suspended over this empty space where you'd hear the Rhine bubbling if the train stopped, if our song stopped.

✳

The rumbling of the bridge has faded away, and our song with it.

✳

And now the single man that we were together, standing in the wagon, this man sits down at one go and cries, like a child. All these men are children, crying. Ridiculously united in tears as we had been in song.

There's nothing to be done. No one can do anything. No one holds back.

✳

Have they cracked up in the other wagons too?

It's a long time before the bodies are back in their customary posture, silent, the tearful spasms over.

The train continues on its way.

No one speaks.

The scenery goes by without us.

For several hours no one has been at the skylight. It must be night time.

There is nothing more to see but the faceless darkness. But there's less lack of air. The stink is less onerous although it's still intense. We stretch out as best we can, ready for our third night in this train.

And at this moment a storm breaks, something which with our dry, burnt, painful throats and our poor bodies we had stopped believing in. A storm. Water. Water again, after all this time.

Heaven hasn't quite forgotten us.

Not the Heaven of the scriptures, the one with a capital H, the boastful one still swaggering inside the heads of some, but the heavens, the sky with clouds, the sky that saturates, the sky whose downpours have the power to save, the only heaven we believe in now.

Which I believe in.

I don't know about the others.

I don't know about anyone but myself.

What I also know is that everyone is getting up, even those who had dropped off to sleep.

We've remembered the lesson of the day before yesterday's rain, and we understand the instinct that without us realising it made us hang on to the precious cardboard cartons of the Red Cross. Thanks to them we collect the water dripping miraculously from all the gaps, all the holes made in the despair and the madness of the first day. Holes where sometimes you seem to be able to see the mark of a tooth.

By chance the comrades in this wagon have managed to enlarge them more skilfully than we did in my first wagon. Did they have a better method? Did they have better tools? Or did they simply take advantage of softer wood, not so dry, not so old? Whatever, water is dripping in, we can see it dripping and filling up the cartons. However quickly we drink it, we have time to savour the joy of watching it dripping before we drink, to watch a small quantity collecting which our hands and our eyes can delight in before our throats swallow it in one go, and we stretch out our hands again towards the roof or the wall. Some even dare to thrust their arms outside; nothing happens, no rifle shot, just water running in and the cartons filling up, and the unbelievable joy of being able to drink a little, and a little more, and a little more. It's raining so hard that the soldiers aren't thinking of anything but sheltering from it.

Unless they're just tired of torturing us.

But that's not very likely.

For the first time in hours, I'm cold. For the first time I go to sleep without being thirsty.

I sleep.

I don't dream.

I'm nowhere.

I wake as the sun rises above the sodden fields of the night. I wake and make my way between the bodies of my comrades. One of them, the only one I see standing and who perhaps has not slept, leaves me his place at the skylight and goes to lie down where I had been. In the gloom of the dawning day I examine this unfamiliar land. The countryside passes beneath my gaze, then houses with indistinct colours. Germany. It isn't anything like I expected, like I imagined. Strange impression of being out of place.

My place? . . . Do I still have a place?

We arrive at a station. My comrades aren't stirring, as if they've decided not to wake up in this hated country. God knows, we would have preferred never to know it. Ill met—an encounter with the real, so greatly feared.

What I thought was a station is no longer really one. Alone at the skylight I look at its bombed-out booking hall, its smashed platforms. I can't help relishing this disaster as if it were a small victory given to me in this ominous dawn, to me as I stand whilst others still sleep. Whilst those in the front wagons sleep an eternal sleep.

No, they're not sleeping. That's just words.

They're rotting.

I try to think only about the ruins.

On a board held up by a single nail I read: Karlsruhe. I know that Karl is Charles. I know that "Ruhe" means "Shut up". I know that from hearing it so often when our moans and groans were disturbing our guards.

Strange for a town to be called "Shut up Charles".

We pass the station and ruins after ruins appear. I have the sudden thought that if we could manage to jump out of the train we might be able to hide amongst these ruins. Futile thought. Futile hope. Obliterate it from the map, like these houses. We're in Germany for good and none of that makes sense any more. I tell myself now that these ruined houses are our own bodies, our own ruin, and sadness mingles with the joy I felt at first. The war is nearly at an end, but so are we. I see myself dying in this fragmented land, in this flattened town which reminds me of so many others. I'm surprised now by the feeling of similarity, so different from what I was feeling just now. I needed all this time, all this suffering, to understand it. Perhaps there is no difference between us and those who live in this land. Nothing resembles a ruin so much as another ruin. Nothing resembles a burnt body so much as another burnt body, a headless body as another headless body, a lifeless, wordless, motionless body as another inanimate body.

Suddenly I remember the face of the man in the rue des Saussaies.

❈

135

I can't think about him for long though; something has hit the wagon a few centimetres away from my face. Before I realise it, a pebble bangs into the barbed wire then hits me full in the cheek. I instinctively crouch down before realising it's a group of children who were looking at me; they're taking advantage of the train's short stop to stone the enemies of Germany. I hear their shouts, I hear without believing: "Juden! Juden! Alle ins Krematorium!" And stones are falling onto my comrades as they sleep whilst I watch, crouching, my cheek bleeding—two, three, four stones banging into the opposite wall, bouncing off and dropping with a thud, followed by a wail. Fortunately, the train moves off, leaving the flood of hatred to pour over the wagons behind. It's woken the comrades. I'm the one who got the worst of it. The others were hardly touched, just a big bump which dragged them from the fitful sleep in which they had taken refuge.

My cheek is burning, just beneath the eye. My neighbour pulls my hands apart to look at the wound.

"It doesn't look too deep."

"The barbed wire slowed it down."

"Bastard krauts."

"They were children."

"Bastard krauts."

"Yes."

He grabs a handkerchief which he'd hung on a hook in the roof. The cloth is still soaked from the night's storm. He makes a compress and my burning cheek is soothed a little by the moisture and the cold.

"Thanks, old man."

"Bastard krauts."

"Yes."

That's all he can say. I don't know what to reply. Deep down, I agree.

And to think I was beginning to feel sympathy for them. That'll teach me.

Between them and us there's nothing in common, that's what this stone is telling me.

Between them and us, the stone and the ruins. Blood and ruins. Only that. Nothing else. Or what if there is something?

Whilst I mull over my anger with them, with myself, with intransigent fate, the others are shaking themselves, as if the clock has chimed for our last day. For I understand, as do all those who are lining up to take their place, carefully, at the skylight where I was standing just now, I understand from remembering those ruins that today will be our last in the wagon. We're coming to the end of the journey.

❀

The train is bowling along on the rails now. No one to slow it down, no more resistance fighters, no more "terrorism". Nothing to stop its journey.

Yes, there are one or two more stations, one or two more stops for technical reasons, but we sense that it won't be long. We pass Stuttgart, Augsburg, more stones being thrown, more shouts of hatred. Fists shaken. Strained looks. But also some who turn away, embarrassed—so says a comrade, though I'm not inclined to believe it.

When my turn to look out comes around again, it must be after ten o'clock. We're passing a town with high yellow walls, walls covered in writing, hoardings, notices without end. No more ruins, alas. Just these large letters which don't mean anything to me, except for the odd word here and there, a name lost in my memory. My initial anxiety comes back to me, reading these strange words. I understand nothing of this language, yet it echoes in the language of my forefathers.

The blood has dried on my cheek and made a scab.

In the wagon no one has died since Bar-le-Duc, as if death had taken what it was owed on the first day, as if death was no longer hungry and a little would be enough. Unlike us. For we're still hungry—we've eaten nothing since yesterday's soup—thirsty—despite the night's rain—this hunger, this thirst which haven't left us since the first day. We're hungry, thirsty, we stink almost as much as the carcasses journeying with us, but we're still alive.

I look at my comrades. I look at them so I can remember this day, this last day, so as never to forget what we looked like at the end of this journey. In the dim light I can see their shaggy heads, their vacant expressions, their unnaturally wide eyes, their ruined bodies. This detritus that we've become.

What are they going to do with us? What can they do with us? There's nothing to be made of us. We serve no purpose. We are nothing. Ghosts. Already, we're fading away. Already, we're no longer there.

München. Munich. Gone midday.

My birthday.

The train waits.

The train reverses.

The train sets off again.

Still nothing to eat.

Another hour's journey.

Someone mentions Dachau.

The train stops.

Yes, it says Dachau.

The door opens to the yelling of men and the barking of dogs.

Today I'm twenty-two.

Is that a large candle smoking over there, that I'll have to blow out?

Today I'm twenty-two, and I'm not quite dead.